GW00854513

# The -30- Press Quarterly
# Issue One

Copyright © 2017 by -30- Press LLC

All rights reserved.

This book or any portion thereof may not be reproduced in any manner whatsoever without the express written permission of the publisher except for the use of brief quotations in a book review.

*Cover design by xaapje*

*Interior design by Ashley Franz Holzmann*

*Edited by Ashley Franz Holzmann*

30press.com

For the community of Nosleep.

———

# Table of Contents

# Introduction From The Editors

---

Hey, everyone. It's lovely to meet you and welcome to the first of what will be many collections of some of the best horror coming out of the up-and-coming writers in the horror community.

My name is Ashley, and I am the Chief Operations Officer of -30- Press. I took the lead on organizing the hard copy of this anthology, which you are now holding in your beautifully soft hands. You must use lotion.

All jokes aside, this is the start of something really exciting for us at -30- Press. For those who have not been following our slow ascent, we are a relatively new publishing company made up of authors. Our goal is to be there for our fellow writers, and to be a force for good in the writing community. We are beginning with horror, but hope to branch out in the coming years.

I am merely a part of a trio, which also consists of Raff, our Chief Executive Officer, and Jake, our Chief Science Officer (he insists on this title). We all come from solid educational backgrounds and have each published books in our own right. This is the beginning, so there will be some growing pains. Thank you for joining us this early. Know that we care deeply about this endeavor and that as time passes, we will pump more and more effort into our publications. We're on a very tight budget, but as we grow we will be investing in our team and our authors heavily.

What we hope to see -30- Press become is a platform and stepping stone for authors to become literary giants. If that's with us directly, excellent; if it means we are helping answer all of the questions newly self-published authors have while they trudge through the processes, we think that's just as important. I also cannot forget to mention our amazing backbone group of staffers hiding in the bushes. Jake, Raff and I have an amazing team of totally non-serial killers helping us with our social media and the website stuff. Without them, -30- Press is just a few words on a blank page.

This is issue one of what will become a quarterly publication. Hopefully this goes without saying, but just to cover all of our bases, this is a collection of short horror stories.

We do not believe in censorship, and some portions of this anthology may disturb or depress you. I thought about briefly introducing each of the stories, but I do not believe I would do any of them justice. The skill of our authors is excellent in this issue, and we could not be more happy to represent them in this anthology. Please click on their websites and social media pages. Find their other books and help support budding writers on their journeys.

If you find yourself completing this book and having enjoyed the experience, we ask that you please take a few minutes to leave us a review. Every review truly helps.

There are going to be moments when you're reading this and you may have to take a step back, or put the book down for a moment. Stuff will get intense. You may not be the same afterwards. Good luck.

Ashley Franz Holzmann
Chief Operations Officer
-30- Press
January, 2017
30Press.com

# The Pancake Family

# By AA Peterson

———————

That pale, huh? Jesus, I bet I look like a ghost. I feel like I've bled out two gallons.

What? No. Not a scratch.

Sorry to ramble. It's just that I'm... what's the word for it?

Detached.

Strange feeling. Seen it enough times in the field. Sort of figured if I was ever going to experience it myself then I would have experienced it by now. Hell of a thing. I feel like I'm floating outside of my body. Just cut the cord and I'd float away.

Did you see the crime scene?

Don't.

Don't look at the pictures. Don't even touch the file. You'll thank me.

I can't get my knees to stop rattling. Is that why you're

holding onto your coffee like that? I'm shaking the table, aren't I? Hold on a second, let me back up my chair. There, that's better.

*INTERVIEWER: We've got to go official now, Hob. Can you confirm for the record that you're waiving your right to an attorney?*

No, I'm still not interested in an attorney.

I mean, yes, I'm waiving my rights.

Sorry.

And I'm as sound of mind as I'll ever be.

*INTERVIEWER: Are you sure?*

Yes.

*INTERVIEWER: Let the record show that Detective Hobson Milgate, retired, has waived his right to an attorney.*

I won't need a lawyer after the DA stops puking and considers taking it public.

They're not showing that to a jury.

*INTERVIEWER: Are you ready to begin?*

No, but I'll talk anyway.

*INTERVIEWER: What led you to the crime scene on the night in question?*

Would you believe I was planning a fishing trip before this started?

Never mind.

Hold on, I'm thinking.

Hard to organize it.

Never been on this side of the interrogation table

before.

I guess it started with the reporter. Name of Bamer. She contacted me a week ago by email and claimed she had new information on the Driscoll murders. I was the lead investigator. The case had gone unsolved for twenty years. Cold as ice.

Frankly, I thought it was all bullshit at first.

You know how that can be. Most of the time it's not even on purpose. Everyone thinks they know something that will crack a case wide open. Theories are easy when you don't have to check them against evidence. The Driscoll murders were a big story around these parts. Lots of interest. Lots of press. Over the years, I must've gotten a couple hundred shit theories.

When I retired, I handed the investigation over to Detective Caroll, but I didn't want him to be bothered. I know he's busy with the recent gang activity. I figured I'd check it out as a courtesy. I wasn't expecting it to go anywhere.

I met her for lunch at Puryear's Cafe. Good-looking blonde gal, professional, so she didn't fit the typical profile of a hoaxer or conspiracy theorist. Not that I put too much faith in profiles. She also might have been one of those creepy gals that gets off on death. God knows I've dealt with those, too.

I still thought she might be pulling my leg, or maybe she had been fooled too, but she had a file with her.

Looked legit. It contained what appeared to be a confession by the Driscoll… well, he wasn't a murderer was he?

I really do wish he had been, you know.

It would have been so much better for everyone.

*INTERVIEWER: Can you please fill us in on the relevant details of the Driscoll case?*

Let's see, it would have been twenty years ago now. Thinking of all those years… I mean, twenty goddamn years. That's a long time to be…

*INTERVIEWER: Take your time, Hob.*

Thanks.

[Throat Clearing]

The Driscolls were a family of six out in the suburbs. Upper middle class. Father was an attorney, mother ran her own business selling pottery out of the house. Four children, all high school age and below. Good kids. Honor roll. No criminal records to speak of. The oldest son was caught smoking dope at his high school once, but nothing much besides that. Just the typical stuff you find when you look at people too closely.

They disappeared October 13th, 1994. No trace was found of the bodies. The mystery and seeing as how it was right around Halloween is probably why the press went so crazy. You still see it show up on some of those unsolved mystery shows. A whole family disappeared and no one saw a thing. No one knew where they went.

A neighbor lodged a sound complaint, which is how we got involved. There was an alarm going off and they figured it might be an intruder or something. We dispatched a vehicle. When no one answered the door, the patrolman went in to investigate.

There were obvious signs of a struggle in the youngest daughter's bedroom. The bed had been flipped over and the sheets were torn. The alarm was a carbon monoxide detector. We found elevated concentrations of carbon monoxide in the fabric of all the bedspreads except the youngest daughter's. We wouldn't have known to look without the alarm.

The neighbor indicated the alarm had been sounding for over a day, and he'd been unable to get anyone to answer the door during that time. We also found several aluminum canisters and some hoses in a dumpster a few blocks away. At the time, we assumed the Driscolls had been gassed and disposed of at a different location. Except the daughter who woke up and put up a struggle.

The investigation gave no leads.

Of course, our first thought was that the father did it. We checked it out but he didn't have motive. No leads to follow up on. Same with the mother. Surviving family checked out clean, too. The father had a few clients who might have had motive, but the means weren't there. He was a divorce lawyer, but not for anybody who could have taken out an entire family without leaving evidence. There was a chemistry teacher who lived three blocks away and we investigated him for a bit because of the canisters but he alibied out. Same with a dentist who lived nearby. The wife had an online flirtation with some kid out in England but nothing adulterous and he wasn't even in the country at the time of the murder.

We settled, unhappily, on the idea of a random killing. Hardest pieces of shit to catch when there's no pattern like that. We must have sunk tens of thousands of man hours into this case, chasing down leads. Nothing ever came of any of it.

We did track down the canisters. They were stolen from a laboratory ten miles away. There was no security footage. We couldn't find any leads on the thief. After six months with no repeat attacks the investigation went cold.

The Driscolls had been knocked out and abducted. Like I said, no one ever found the bodies. Who was to say they hadn't just run off?

Until, well, I'd rather only talk about that once.

*INTERVIEWER: What can you tell us about how the confession wound up with Miss Bamer?*

She'd been following the case for some years, both personally and as a reporter. Like I said, it captured the imagination of a lot of people. Even seemingly normal folks thought it could have been aliens, ghosts or demons. Miss Bamer published a retrospective on the murders given the twenty year anniversary. It caused a renewed interest, which happened from time to time. As usual, I declined to comment citing lack of new evidence. I remembered her asking for my quote though, which is why I accepted the lunch meeting.

After publication of the article, Miss Bamer claimed that she had been sent a file. She wished to have me authenticate. The most pertinent part of the file was a confession. I assured Miss Bamer that such false documents are not uncommon, especially on older cases like this, and that I'd personally heard two dozen confessions of the Driscoll murders. She was insistent. Once I felt she wasn't trying to pull off a hoax or getting off on the idea of talking about a murder, I agreed to the meeting.

She stated the confession had been mailed to her in the same envelope she showed to me when we met for lunch.

*INTERVIEWER: Can you describe its contents?*

Old newspaper clippings outlining the progress of my investigation. They seemed appropriately yellowed, so I'd guess they were from the trophy book of the perpetrator. There were also six photos alleging to be of the individual members of the Driscoll family, as well as several other photos of the... facility where they had been taken.

Look at that.

My hands won't stop shaking, see? I'm trying as hard as I can and I just can't make it happen. I'll have to ask the paramedic for a sedative when I'm done with the statement. I don't think I'll be able to sleep, otherwise.

No, I'm fine for now. I don't want anything to interfere with my recollection for your recording.

Just carrying it around in my head is like... sorry, I'll stay focused.

The photos were of the Driscoll family, of course. At the time I didn't know that. The photos had aged poorly and they could have been of anyone. It was very hard to distinguish features. However, given the elaborate nature of the file I figured it did warrant a further look.

As to the confession letter, well, it was brief. It gave an address. That's the first thing I noticed. I couldn't locate the address online, which meant it had to be old. The confession letter said, 'Stop printing lies. I never killed anyone. It just took a while to get them ready for breakfast.' There was no signature.

I just remembered something.

God damnit.

We got sent a breakfast menu a month after the disappearance! Someone had drawn a red circle around a picture of pancakes. The letter said 'They're not dead, they're getting ready for breakfast!' We put it in the junk lead file.

Oh God.

*INTERVIEW: Detective Milgate, do you need a moment?*

Oh God.

I... how could I have known?

We tried to track down that menu. We could never find out where it had come from. It wasn't any place local. The identifying information had been cut out.

I don't know what else we could have done.

I just... dear God.

*INTERVIEWER: Why did you decide to personally investigate the location mentioned in the letter?*

Sorry.

I wanted to make sure it wasn't a hoax. Part of me still wasn't convinced. I've had twenty years of people sending me fake evidence. I guess maybe the case captured my imagination, too. I always figured one day I'd think of something I'd overlooked and solve the whole thing. Felt unbelievable to have someone dump the answer in my lap. I needed to see with my own two eyes.

Miss Bamer had pinpointed the location with city records, but neither of us was sure if it was still there. It was an abandoned industrial building. The last time it had a valid mailing address was fifty years ago. It might have caved in for all we knew.

I think I also wanted to be the one to crack it. Whether or not it was dumped in my lap. That case has hung over my head for twenty years.

Miss Bamer and I agreed to meet there the following morning.

*INTERVIEWER: Can you describe the crime scene?*

13

Yes.

It was an industrial building, as I stated. Approximately one hundred twenty feet long by maybe forty-five feet wide. It was a wooden structure and at first the condition seemed to match the neighboring buildings, however I noticed the facade had been recently patched in a few locations. Further investigation also revealed that the entrance had been chained and locked. My understanding was that it used to be a sheet metal shop. At least… excuse me, is there a garbage can?

I might vomit.

Thank you.

We.

[Gagging]

Sorry.

I thought I was empty.

No, I want to get this done with. Then I'm going to want that sedative.

I could smell something from inside the building. Very faintly. I figured that would count as probable cause, not that I need it as a civilian, but you never forget the way a corpse smells.

They were… bad enough they had that same smell.

I hadn't forgotten how to pick a lock, so I let myself inside.

You know, I really do wish they had been corpses. I really do wish he had been a serial killer. I really do.

Please say you believe me.

*INTERVIEWER: I do. Can you describe the interior of the building?*

I'm trying to focus through this. I really am. I'm sorry, it's just that I'd like to go to sleep after this for a very long time.

Is the paramedic here? Is the sedative ready?

Thank goodness.

The warehouse had not been as abandoned as we were previously led to believe. The interior had a hallway with six rooms. The construction was old but visibly newer than the rest of the building. The walls between each room had been soundproofed. There were no windows to the outside or doorways between the rooms themselves. The only access was through the hallway.

I tried to make Miss Bamer leave at that point.

You see… the smell was stronger inside.

You could feel it. The smell. Like a grit getting stuck in your nose. Like bits of sand all over your skin.

The rooms, uh, the rooms contained presses. Hydraulic presses. Four foot by eight foot custom presses. I couldn't figure out what they were at first, because they were hovering over what looked like hospital beds. There were IV bags in each room as well as other medical equipment.

That's how he kept them alive for so long, of course.

I think I might be seeing black spots.

*INTERVIEWER: Do you need to take a break?*

The idea of having to start this again is worse than the idea of finishing it.

*INTERVIEWER: Then please describe your next course of action.*

The building was obviously an active crime scene. I had no doubt at this point. I was in the lair of what I believed to be a serial killer.

I tried to tell Miss Bamer to leave several times. She refused on the grounds that it would not be right to leave me on my own. There wasn't much time to make an issue out of it. My opinion of her was that she was a bit nosey but basically alright and I didn't think she'd be a liability if she stayed out of my way. I had to make a judgment call as to whether or not I should proceed on my own in case the family was somehow, impossibly, still alive and perhaps in danger or if I should leave and call for back-up.

I had told my wife where I was going previously so I knew my absence would be noted and reported if the worst happened. Neither of us could get cell phone reception.

Sorry, I'm rambling.

It was then that I heard… not even a gasp. It was like a gasp, but not really. I don't want to describe it anymore than that.

There was a sound. It drew my attention further on. I had to act. That's all the matters.

There were some stairs at the very far end of the warehouse descending into a basement. I told Miss Bamer to remain behind and pulled my service revolver. I had a flashlight on my person as well, and turned it on as I descended into the basement.

The basement had been hand dug. Maybe even over the course of the entire twenty year disappearance. I don't know. The floor was dirt and there was a tunnel that retreated back far enough that it had to be supported with struts at regular intervals. When my flashlight first illuminated the... stack...

I wish they'd been dead.

I wish he'd been a serial killer.

*INTERVIEWER: Please take a moment.*

After I... after I recovered my first thought was 'Thank God, they are all dead.'

[Gagging]

I'm sixty-four years old for Christ's sake. I'm not a young man who can forget things anymore. When you're young you have this sense that you're invincible and that you're never going to die. I don't have that to protect me anymore.

Look at me whining, when they had that done to them.

It's my fault. I should have found them. Saved them, somehow.

*INTERVIEWER: I'm sorry, Hob, I've got to ask. Can you*

*describe the scene?*

Yeah—

[Gagging]

I can.

I didn't know what I was looking at, at first. Hell, I still don't. It was… well, it was a stack. Maybe two feet thick. From the stink and coloring it was obviously made of flesh. I thought maybe he'd hacked them up and stacked them up in pieces. That would have been bad enough. The first thing that alerted me to the truth was the eyeball. On the top of the stack was a perfectly round eyeball in the middle of a socket that had been distorted to the size of a saucer. That's when I realized what I was looking at was…

Twenty goddamn years of torture, basically.

He had the entire Driscoll family under those presses for twenty years, keeping them alive on an IV drip, increasing the pressure on them so very slowly that their bodies had time to adapt, until they'd been flatted like… well, like pancakes. He squished them by about a quarter inch every year for twenty years. Then he'd pulled them out when they were too broken and wretched to move, without any chance of recovery and stacked them on top of each other. I've got no idea what for. I don't want to know.

And I was still thinking "Thank God they're all dead" when the one on top started gasping again.

*INTERVIEWER: What did they say?*

Nothing at first. It couldn't speak without help. I think… it would have been Avery Driscoll. Not that I could tell much about the gender or the age. But the hair was blonde where there was hair. The head was a mess of scars. I think the son of a bitch who did this must have removed parts of their skulls. I've got no idea how he got their heads so flat, otherwise. Not as flat as the rest of the bodies but flat. Who the hell knows how their brains handled that. Their lips were punctured by teeth everywhere, after the presses had flattened out their noses, I guess.

Avery was fourteen when he disappeared.

I've stopped shaking.

Goddamn weird the way our bodies work, isn't it?

What else?

There was a machine. A sort of pump. I followed a hose with my flashlight and realized everyone in the stack was hooked up to the pump. I don't think they could breathe on their own, you see. Not after a while. There simply wasn't enough volume for their lungs to inflate. There was some sort of opening cut right into each of their chests. There was a switch on the pump. I don't know why I pressed it. I was in a panic. I wanted to do something. Maybe some stupid part of me thought that if I switched it on they would inflate and be okay.

I switched it. It increased the volume of air to the topmost hose. I could hear the pump working harder.

Which is when Avery Driscoll started to scream.

He begged me to kill him. He said other things too. He didn't make much sense. Kept yelling 'Bane of Error' over and over again. Something about 'the Family' too. Didn't understand it. He was in pain and I would hope he had gone insane several years previously.

*INTERVIEWER: Oh my God.*

My thoughts exactly.

I didn't know what to do. He wouldn't stop screaming. I believe he was convinced I was his torturer. A closer look at his eye revealed that it was mostly a mess of white scar tissue. He was as blind as a bat.

You know, I spoke with some burn victims once. They told me that they managed to find meaning and purpose again after a while. I don't know how anyone in the Driscoll family could have done that.

I stated my name. I told him I was a detective. I told him I was there to help. I repeated it over and over again, knowing of course there was nothing that anyone anywhere could do to help.

Miss Bamer arrived, drawn by the sound. Before she saw the stack she told me that I had screamed and she had come to help, but I do not remember having done so. Nevertheless she arrived. Then she saw the stack and screamed but I was intent on Avery Driscoll. He was able to hear. He became lucid for a few moments. It was a strain to understand what he said, but I will never be able to forget it.

"Please kill me. It hurts. I don't want to be a monster. Please kill me and tell my family I died a long time ago. I don't know if they're still looking for me. Don't let them know what happened to me. Please kill me."

He could still cry and he did, although his tear ducts were too deformed for it to be noticeable.

I should have forced Miss Bamer to leave. That is the only action in the matter which I regret more than failing to solve the case twenty years ago. Not just for her own sake, but for what she did next. I don't think she could have wounded them anymore deeply if she'd tried. She took away the last comfort any of them in that stack had.

You see, they had not been able to speak to one another for twenty years.

She said, "That's all of them isn't it? That's the entire Driscoll family. They're all alive in there. The whole family."

For twenty years, each member of the Driscoll family had been unaware their fellow inmates were the other members of their family. They'd all been holding out hope their family was okay. All of them dreaming someone out there loved them and was free from suffering.

Do you know what the screams of six people tortured over two decades, smashed down to a width of four inches sounds like when they're all stacked on top of one another?

It sounds like the gates of hell swinging open.

*INTERVIEWER: I think that is enough, Detective Milgate.*

Not yet.

It was my mistake. I should have tried harder. Tracked down that lead. Maybe that's what they meant, screaming that. It was my error so it was my responsibility.

I shot them. Mercy is hard, but I owed it to them. I am the one that failed to save them.

It only took one bullet to go all the way through. I emptied my revolver, though. To make sure they didn't linger. To give them that final peace.

It was the only kindness I had to give them.

We left and called for back-up after that. Neither Miss Bamer nor I wished to remain with the bodies. I elected not to follow the crime scene investigators back into the basement. I asked if I could make my statement and leave and after one of them saw what I had seen they agreed.

May I have my sedative now?

*INTERVIEWER: Yes… yes, of course.*

Thank you.

Please show in the paramedic. I'll roll up my sleeve. My wife has diabetes so I'm well aware of the routine. Oh, and please make sure you have the same courtesy available for Miss Bamer. She seemed to have it worse than me, after. Poor woman couldn't even throw up or cry.

*INTERVIEWER: Of course. Do you know where she is now? She told the lead at the crime scene she was going home but we haven't been able to reach her.*

Did you try the paper?

*INTERVIEWER: Which paper?*

The Daily World.

*INTERVIEWER: Are you sure? There is no one by the last name of Bamer on staff with the Daily World.*

# Pebbles

# By Max Lobdell

---

We thought we were having a hell of a hailstorm when we woke up in the middle of the night to a peal of thunder and the sound of our cabin being pelted. It went on for about a minute, then it stopped. There wasn't any rain, which was strange. We went back to sleep, faintly aware of the smell of something burning. I figured it was probably from a lightning strike somewhere else.

In the morning, we realized how wrong we'd been. Jill was the first to get up, but her yelling ensured I was right on her heels.

Our property was a wreck. Baseball-sized burns covered the lawn as far as we could see, and when I went outside to assess the damage to our cabin, I was dismayed to find similar, albeit smaller, burns all over the roof.

"Had to have been meteorites," Jill claimed. "I bet that thunder we heard was a big one breaking up."

I didn't know enough to disagree, but I thought it was pretty weird. She concurred.

We spent the day doing our best to rake up the marble-sized pieces of rock, which we hauled out and piled in the back of the property by the compost heap. Jill thought they might be worth something to someone, so we were going to bring a jar full back home at the end of the summer.

As she talked, I could tell she was uncomfortable. The work we'd been doing had aggravated the chapped skin around her mouth and under her arms. Something about the time of year always did it to her, and no matter how much she tried to keep the areas moist, they would still crack painfully. I told her I'd finish up for the night if she wanted to go inside. She did.

I made a vague plan to excise the ruined bits of lawn and reseed it, but I soon got frustrated. It was going to be a major project that would take days, if not weeks. There were still whole areas of the yard where we hadn't picked up the meteorites, but they'd wreck the lawnmower if I tried to go over them just to make the area presentable in the meantime. Such a pain in the ass.

The next day, to make matters worse, we noticed the well water had acquired a taste. It was briny and flat; almost coppery. Wholly unpleasant. We could drink bottled water for the rest of the vacation, which we'd been doing most of the time anyway, but we still showered and brushed our teeth with the stuff that came out of the well. And for a while, we kept doing it. On the bright side, my gums had stopped bleeding when I flossed. Must've been all the extra minerals from the well water that gets filtered out in municipal reservoirs.

After another long day of yard work, I was preparing dinner when I heard Jill shriek from the bathroom. She'd gone in to take a shower a few minutes earlier. When I rushed in to see what was wrong, she was coughing and swearing and working to wipe away clear, viscous something that had pooled on her face. I could see the shower head oozing the same stuff, clogging the drain and puddling like syrup on the bottom of the bathtub. If she hadn't leapt out the second she felt it hit her face, she would've been covered from head to toe.

I helped Jill towel off as much of the stuff as I could, and a minute or two later, the shower head had started spitting out water again. It took a bit of coaxing, but she eventually held her head under its flow so she could wash her hair of the residue or whatever the hell had gotten on her.

Once Jill was as clean as she was going to get, I called the guy in charge of well maintenance for the county. The only guy in charge of well maintenance for the county. He answered right away, but gave the reply I knew was coming: It'd be at least three weeks before he could get out here and take a look. I pleaded with him to make some time to come earlier, and offered him way too much money, but the best he could do was move the appointment ahead by two days.

He told me that he'd seen algae blooms in a few of the local wells. The only suggestion he had was to run the water until it looked normal, which is what we'd done during our subsequent showers. I hated having to wait, but it was good to know he'd seen something like this before.

Over dinner, Jill and I tried to come to an agreement about what to do. I wanted to go home. There wasn't any reason why we needed to keep putting up with the weird water and the yard work when we could go home, be comfortable, and hire people to take care of it all.

Jill wanted to stay. She'd been looking forward to this trip for months, and the chapped skin on her mouth was feeling much better. The cabin had belonged to her parents and she'd spent many summers here. No matter how unpleasant the circumstances might have gotten for us, they were still less stressful than all the work she had waiting for her when we were scheduled to return home in two months.

I caved.

Yesterday morning, we woke up to a remarkably pleasant surprise. In the parts of the yard where we hadn't carted away the meteorites, the burned parts had disappeared. When I went outside to look, I saw the burns were covered in the same viscous stuff that would occasionally come from our pipes. Underneath the ooze was healthy, green grass. When I looked closer, I saw ants —ants almost too small to see—were crawling up and down the blades and carrying away dried pieces of the slime to bring back to their homes.

I headed back inside and told Jill. She acted happy to hear it, but I could tell she was deeply uncomfortable. The chapped skin around her mouth and nose had gotten bad again. I offered to take her to the clinic in town, but she didn't want to sit in the car for four hours just to have the doctor give her the same cream she'd been using on herself for the last week. While she spoke, the left corner of her mouth cracked open and spilled a thin rivulet of blood down her chin.

Sighing with exasperation, she grabbed a paper towel, turned on the sink to wet it, and put the paper against her wound. When she sat back down, I saw the faucet was drooling the sticky algal slime that'd caused her the problem in the first place. But it was too late. She'd already pressed it to the crack in her skin.

Before I could mention this to her, Jill's eyes had brightened. She pulled the paper towel away, a string of syrupy fluid still connecting the towel to her face. The cut was gone.

"Don't," I told her.

Jill didn't listen. She went back to the sink and turned it on. Sticky, clear stuff flowed. She filled her hands and

29

brought the contents to her face. She rubbed for a moment, then turned back toward me.

Behind the sheen around her mouth and nose was new, healthy skin.

"Pretty cool!" Jill exclaimed, and wiped the residue away. I didn't know what to think, let alone say. I figured some homeopathic doctor who minored in algae studies would find it completely normal.

We went to bed and slept. In the morning, Jill's mouth and nose, while much better than they'd been at their worst, were still not as perfect as they were right after she'd applied the slime. I told her I was going to go out in the yard and do some more work.

Before I could get out of bed, though, she kissed me. Now, we're in our late 50s. We're affectionate with one another, don't get me wrong, but most of the time we just cuddle on the couch and share a pizza. It's easier that way. Requires fewer blue pills, too. That's not to say we don't have a sex life, because we do, but it's more of a once-every-two-months kind of thing.

Jill's rapturous kiss was less like one from the woman to whom I'd been married for 35 years and more like that of the teenager she was when we first started dating. I didn't bother concerning myself with that particular difference, though. I followed her lead and we did what apparently needed to be done. No blue pills required, thank you very much.

Afterward, while I got dressed, I told Jill I was going to start raking up the meteorites we'd left the other day. She didn't pay attention. She wanted me back in bed. I laughed and reminded her that even when we were kids I still had the refractory period of a climate cycle. She nodded and told me to be safe outside, then made an obvious show of slipping her hands under the blankets. She looked amazing. To my surprise, I felt renewed stirring below my belt. Before I could say "fuck it" and jump back into bed, though, I shook my head. I really needed to get going on that yard work. It was starting to cloud up and I didn't want to have to put it off because of rain. I told Jill to have fun, then went outside.

In the untouched area of the yard, the grass was ankle-high. All the burns were gone. Clumps of slime still sat in the grass. The ants that'd been going crazy for the stuff were nowhere to be found.

I raked and raked and raked. The pebbles piled up and I shoveled them into the wheelbarrow and brought them to the main pile by the compost heap. I was a little surprised there were no ants at all. I could see their anthills bored into the ground all over the place, but not a single one was out and about.

I'd been working for about two hours nonstop, so during a break, while I chugged from my bottle of water, I bent down to get a closer look at the spots where the ants had swarmed the other day. Something was there that I hadn't noticed while I was raking. Something definitely not there when I looked the previous day.

There were infinitesimal white dots coating the same blades of grass that'd been crawling with ants less than 24 hours ago. I plucked a few blades from the ground and held them in front of my face, hoping to get a better view. The dots were slightly ovoid in shape. Something clicked. Eggs. The ants must've had such a massive meal of that slime stuff that it drove them to reproduce like crazy. Or something. I have no idea how they make ants.

I heard raindrops impacting the trees on the other side of the property, and ten seconds later, they reached me. A distant bolt of lightning streaked the sky, and thunder boomed a moment later. Sighing, I put the rake and shovel in the wheelbarrow and wheeled it all back to the shed. More lightning and thunder. I figured I wouldn't be getting anything else done around the yard until the storm passed.

I headed back into the cabin, banged my boots against the doorway to get the mud off, and stepped inside.

"Charlie," Jill called. I heard water running in the bathroom.

From the kitchen where I stood, spooning last night's fruit salad into a bowl, I called back, "What's up?"

"Come take a bath with me!"

I laughed to myself. That bathtub could barely fit 110 pound Jill, let alone 250 pound me. I brought my bowl of fruit salad with me down the hall and into the bedroom.

Before I turned the corner to the bathroom, the water was turned off and Jill shouted out again, "Charlie, are you coming?" Her voice sounded a little different. Crisper, somehow.

I stepped into the candle-lit bathroom. Jill was in the tub, leaning back against its curved shape. She was resting her head on a folded towel. She glanced over at me and smiled. Her hands roamed up and down her body.

Even in the dim light, she looked incredible. I didn't know whether it was the prospect of repeating our fun from that morning or just the sight of her touching herself, but it was remarkably enjoyable. I placed my bowl on the sink and started to undress.

A nearby bolt of lightning immediately followed by an explosion of thunder made me jump. As my surprise faded and I continued to take off my clothes, I realized I'd seen something different in the harsh illumination of the lightning.

On the other side of the bathroom, Jill continued her teasing. "Come here and touch me," she whispered. Again, I noticed the unusual quality of her voice. Another clap of thunder shook the house, and that time, the associated burst of lightning showed me exactly what I had trouble identifying after the first strike.

With a gasp, I turned on the light. In the harsh, overhead fluorescence, everything was revealed.

The tub in which Jill bathed was filled to the brim with

clear slime. As I watched, she slid beneath the surface, coating her face and head, and came back up. When she breached the surface, she spoke.

"Please, Charlie, I can't even tell you how good this feels."

Again, the different vocal quality. Now, though, in the harsh light, I saw another change. Her hair. Jill's hair had been gray since her late 40s. It was light brown now.

Jill manipulated herself with her right hand and reached for me with her left. Clear fluid oozed from her hand and arm and puddled on the floor like heavy syrup. "Come feel this with me, Charlie."

I didn't move. Part of me wanted to pull her from the tub, but another part, as the rain pounded against the roof and thunder rattled the windowpanes, was too frightened to touch her. I moved closer, but stayed out of her reach. Standing at the foot of the tub, I stared at my wife as she bucked her hips against her hand and mouthed my name over and over. Ripples in the slime caused it to slosh against the sides of the tub.

"Jill, please get out. Please." My voice trembled and was barely audible over the pouring rain.

She reached for me with both hands and smiled, then spoke. "Don't you want to be young with me again? To start fresh? Don't you remember how good it felt?"

Jill slid down, and I thought she was going to dip under the slime again. But she stopped at her mouth. She opened it and let the slime pool inside. She closed her lips and I saw her throat work as she swallowed the mouthful.

"It feels so right. So perfect. I want to share this with you, sweetheart."

My mind reeled. I thought about every ache and pain I'd accumulated over my 56 years. Every pockmark and hemorrhoid and scaly patch that'd come along over those long decades throbbed, as if wanting to be noticed. Before me was a way to make it stop. I remembered how Jill and I were as teenagers. Full of life and energy and libido; all things that, over the years, had just started to evaporate. I stared at my wife, who looked exactly like she had when she was 25.

Despite my fear, a pang of desire shot through me. Desire and arousal. I wanted Jill. I wanted to be with her in every way imaginable. We could grow old together again—or never grow old at all. Our happiness could last forever if we wanted. All I had to do was join her in the bathtub.

I took a step forward and resumed taking off my clothes. Jill purred and lapped up more of the slime. Some she swallowed, some she drooled from the corners of her mouth. She absentmindedly played with herself while she watched me, apparently delighted I was going to join her in this new, impossible youth.

As I struggled to bend over and take off my socks, something that'd been a pain in my ass since I passed the 225 mark on the scale, I noticed something that caused me to stop. Jill's breasts were shrinking. Before my eyes, her hips slimmed and her pubic hair disappeared. Her feet no longer came to the edge of the tub, but instead barely touched it.

"Come bathe with me, honey." Jill's voice was high and childlike. I recoiled. Whatever was happening to her was going faster. She looked 4 or 5.

"It's incredible," she chirped, again reaching for me with one hand and rubbing herself with the other in an act so obscene in her new, young context, that I turned away, nauseated.

"Charlie," came the tiny voice behind me. I didn't turn around.

"Sweetheart?"

The last word was practically babbled, but still carried with it an element of inquisitiveness, and, no matter how much I try to tell myself otherwise, dejection. She didn't speak again.

A moment later, I turned around. Floating in the tub was a red shape, approximately the size of of a lemon. Tears filled my eyes as it shrank to the size of a cherry, then a pea, then a grain of rice. When I blinked, it was gone. A ribbon of white fluid hung motionless in the slime.

"I'm so sorry, my love," I whispered to it. Distant thunder rolled across the forest.

# Sisters in the Snow:

# My Grandmother's Tail

# By James "DexX" Dominguez

---

It was decades ago, but I remember it like it was yesterday. My sister and I had been fighting again, like we did so often.

This fight got more heated than usual. I screamed an obscenity at my sister before turning to storm out of the room, but then my neck suddenly whipped back painfully and I realized she was yanking my hair. In pain and shock, I spun around and slapped her hard across the face.

We didn't often get physical, but when we did we didn't mess around.

I don't know where it would have ended up, how far the violence would have escalated, but suddenly, there was Nonno. That was what we called my grandmother, on my Dad's side. She had some kind of dementia, and between that and her thick accent from the old country, she rarely spoke. She was a small, pale, brittle ghost that lived on the periphery of my life, hardly making an impression.

This day was an exception. Showing sudden fierceness, she interposed herself between me and my sister and looked back and forth at each of us with an expression of fury on her face. She looked hard at my sister's hand, still entangled in my long hair, and then back at her face. My sister sheepishly let go and dropped her hand to her side.

"Sisters love!" she shouted at us, her voice shedding most of its usual fragility. "Do not do this! Love your sister! Love!"

Suddenly the furious mask cracked, slipped, and dissolved into grief. Where moments before had been an expression of pure anger, there was now nothing but sadness and loss. She clasped her small, wrinkled hands over her mouth, but I could see her pale greyish-brown eyes well with tears.

Without another word, she turned and hurried out of the room as quickly as her arthritic legs would take her, while her shoulders quivered with silent sobs.

My sister and I stared at each other, struck mute by Nonno's double-dip of uncharacteristic anger and uncharacteristic sadness. We stood there, stunned and silent, for maybe twenty seconds, and then I turned and ran after her.

Predictably, Nonno was in the kitchen, making tea. While she was generally quiet and stayed out of trouble, her tea-making habits were a source of conflict in our household. You see, she could never make one cup. Every time she wanted tea, she would make four cups, then drink only one of them while the other three went cold.

My mother was infuriated by the waste. The economy was not in good shape, and my father's job was on the brink of making him redundant. He was hardly paid enough as it was, but if he lost even that meager income, then... well, it was a source of stress for all of us. Looking back, I wonder if that is why my sister and I fought so bitterly: a fear of scarcity.

Sure enough, Nonno was carefully lifting four china teacups down from the cabinet, and as I walked up beside her she placed them carefully in the center of the four saucers that were already on the kitchen bench. I heard a soft clink as the fourth one was put in place.

"Nonno, stop," I said gently. "Why don't you sit down? I'll make you tea. Okay?"

She turned to look at me when I spoke, and I saw her eyes had gone vague and dreamy again, as they were most of the time, but then they sharpened and I could tell she was really seeing me.

"Why do you fight?" she asked softly, and gently placed one of her incredibly soft hands on my cheek. It was cool against my still anger-flushed skin.

I didn't have an answer for her, not back then, so I pressed on. "Sit down, Nonno. Get comfortable," I insisted. "I'll make the tea while you sit and rest."

She threw a worried look down at the four neatly lined up cups, and then looked back at me. Her mouth opened, as if to object, but then, with a nod, she shuffled over to the table, pulled out a chair, and sat down.

I didn't want to cause any kind of scene, so I quickly and carefully put two of the cups and saucers away while she was distracted, then I put the kettle on the stove. I rinsed the old leaves out of the pot, replaced them with fresh leaves from the jar, and then moved closer to Nonno while I waited for the water to boil.

"It'll just be a minute," I said, a little too brightly.

To me, my forced cheerfulness sounded too obvious to be believed, but she smiled up at me. "Thank you, Anna," she said.

I had no idea who Anna was, but I smiled back and humored her. "Nothing like a hot cup of tea to make everything feel better, right Nonno?"

Her smile slipped, and she looked confused, then I saw recognition in her eyes, followed by sadness. "I am sorry, little one," she said, sounding more grounded. "You are not Anna. She is a long time gone. I forget sometimes."

A burbling whine announced that the water was boiled, so I crossed to the stove and twisted the bakelite knob to the off position. "Who is Anna?" I asked, desperate to make some kind of conversation. "Um, who was, Anna, I suppose. Uh. Sorry." Mentally, I was cursing my stupidity, but outwardly I just kept the smile fixed in place and made the tea.

Nonno stayed silent until I brought over the steaming pot, followed by the cups and the tea and milk. With everything in place, I sat down opposite and began to pour out the tea.

"I loved my sisters," she said softly.

"Oh, you had sisters?" I asked, and a blush crept across my face. It was embarrassing to realize that I knew almost nothing about her. I didn't even know she had sisters. That's the kind of thing I should have known, right?

I slid her cup of tea across the green formica tabletop and she stared at it for a long while.

Then she began to tell me a story.

\*\*\*

Anna was the eldest. She was short, but she had a tall heart. You know? Her hair was long and black and curly like yours. I loved her hair. Mine was ugly, I thought; not black, not blonde, not brown, not anything. I envied her glossy black hair.

Next was Slavka. She had a great brain. She would

read and read. We were very poor, and books cost so much money, but she always found books to read somehow. She was very kind to me.

Then, Una. Sweet Una. She was prettiest, but not vain. She was funny, made me laugh and laugh. In another place, she would have been a movie star.

I said we were poor, but life was good enough. Mother was taken by influenza before I was old enough to remember her, but my sisters were my mother. Anna was strong, good at making decisions. Slavka was gentle and caring. Una was fun and playful. Father worked so hard that I barely saw him, and when he was home he was always tired. Together, my sisters raised me.

We might have gone on like that forever if the war had not come. I was too young to understand what it was about. I did not know who our enemies were, and I had no reason to think that not all of the folk in our village were our friends.

To some, you see, we were outsiders. They distrusted our kind, considered us intruders in their land. I was an innocent child and I never realized it, but as the building hatred of war crept across the land, the old mistrust grew into something worse.

It was the middle of winter when the soldiers came. Late one night, Anna woke me, telling me I must be quiet. I heard a murmuring outside, growing louder as I gathered with my sisters in our small kitchen, cold and dark that winter night. Father had not come home from work, so it was just the four of us.

My sisters hissed at me to stay out of sight, but I peeked out of the window. The soldiers were accompanied by a mob of the townsfolk. The baker who sold us our bread every day among them. So was the schoolteacher. They held burning torches and wooden clubs, and their faces were stony, expressionless. The soldiers held guns.

As I watched, they kicked in the door of our neighbors' house and ran inside. There were shouts and screams, then the sharp pop pop pop of gunshots. The shouts and screams stopped, and I heard Una sobbing quietly. Our neighbors were of the same people as us, and as innocent as I was, I understood that we would be next.

Anna took charge, as was her way, bustling us into boots and cloaks and scarves and shawls. We did not have warm overcoats or thick boots, but what choice did we have? As soon as we were ready, Anna led us to the back door. The noise of the mob had gotten louder, and as she lifted the latch as quietly as she could, we heard a banging on the front door.

"Open up traitors!" shouted a taunting voice. "If you co-operate we may just arrest you!"

Without a word, we slipped out into the freezing night. Slavka, clever as always, went back to close the door behind us, so as not to give a clue to our pursuers. Then we were away.

Our house backed onto the woods. In the moonlight, the bare trees were like black skeletons clawing at the sky. The moon was almost full, making the fallen snow glow a ghostly pale blue. Anna led, crunching a path for our little feet through the crunchy snow, then Una and me, and Slavka came behind.

I realized we were heading to Auntie's house. Auntie was once married to my father's older brother, a woodcutter, but he was crushed by a falling tree before they had any children, many years before I was born. As long as I had known her, she had lived alone in a small shack in the woods. Children in our town whispered that she was a witch, but to me she was just Auntie.

The snow crackled and squeaked as we ran, and within minutes my poor tiny feet were numb. My battered hand-me-down shoes were barely adequate to carry me to market and back. In the snow, I was little better than barefoot.

I whined to Anna to give me a piggyback, but she shushed me. I was going to complain again, but then I heard it: voices behind us, *shouting*. Anna tried to increase our speed, but I was slowing the rest of them down. The voices were getting louder, and when I looked back could see a faint orange glow from their torches.

It was clever Slavka who realized they were following our fresh footprints. There was no way we could hide our trail, so she suggested we split up. In a small clearing, she

44

suggested that Anna should take me straight to Auntie, but she and Una should go in two different directions and confuse the mob that was chasing us.

In the moonlight, I could see that Anna was unsure, but time was short and she quickly nodded. "Run around in circles!" she instructed the other two. Don't give them a clear trail. Get to Auntie's as quickly as you can after that."

Una dashed off to our left, her golden curls turned silvery by the moon. I heard Anna whisper, "Please be careful!" Moments later, Slavka was gone as well, heading right.

The cold in my feet could not compare to the icy feeling in my heart as my sisters disappeared into that frosty night. Soon they were lost to my sight, and the sound of their feet swishing through the snow was swallowed up by the trees.

Anna turned to me and asked if I still wanted a piggyback. I nodded enthusiastically, and she knelt down to let me clamber aboard. Then we were away. As I was bounced along, I sank my face into Anna's black ringlets and tried to ignore the sounds of pursuit behind us.

I don't know how long she ran. Endless trees slowly crept behind us, each of them looking the same. None of our surroundings looked familiar, and I hoped Anna remembered the way. Her breathing had become harsh and labored, and halfway up a steep embankment she came to a stop.

She lowered herself onto a fallen tree, old and rotten, and as she panted I could see thick white clouds of vapor puff out of her mouth. I let go of her and stood on the log. Looking back, I could still see a hint of torchlight, but it didn't seem to be any brighter. Slavka's plan seemed to have worked.

I asked if our sisters were going to be okay, and Anna said of course they would. She was a terrible liar, but I pretended to believe her. With nothing else to do, I brushed away a patch of snow and sat down beside her.

We were still sitting there when we heard a gunshot echo through the woods. Faintly, after it, I could hear the mob roar. It no longer sounded like a mass of people; it sounded like a monster, and I suppose that is exactly what it was.

Leaning against Anna for warmth, I felt her jump violently. She jumped to her feet and looked behind, and I heard her breath catch in her throat. "Slavka!" she whispered, and I could sense her despair.

"Slavka is clever!" I declared with a defiant pout. "Those bad men won't catch her."

Anna looked at me. The moon was behind her, so her face was in shadow, but I heard her say, "Of course. Clever Slavka. We'll see her at Auntie's." As I said, she was a terrible liar.

Moments later, there was another gunshot, and then two more in quick succession. These ones clearly came from our left, and closer than the previous one. Muffled by snow and softened by trees, there was still no mistaking the whoops and yells of the men. Even at that young age I understood: they had made a game of hunting us.

Shockingly close, right behind us, we heard a man laugh, then another man laughed in response. They had split into three groups to chase us. Slavka's plan had failed, and some part of the mob was right on our heels.

Anna's head darted from left to right desperately, trying to decide what to do next. Suddenly she seized my wrist. "Into the log!" she whispered. I hadn't noticed that our temporary seat had a small cavity in it.

"I won't fit!" I whispered.

"Yes you will," Anna hissed in reply. "Now, quickly."

Realization dawned. "You won't fit!"

"Without my baby sister on my back, I can run much more quickly," she said. "Please, I'll help you in."

Anna picked me up and pushed me into the rotten hollow feet first. "Help me," she muttered, and I shuffled backwards on my elbows. Anna glanced back where we had come. The voices were getting terribly close.

My head was barely inside the log, but my hips had struck a narrow point and I couldn't slip in any further. Anna declared that it would have to do, then placed a delicate finger on my lips.

"No matter what happens," she whispered fiercely, "stay silent."

"But what about you?" I replied, and I could feel tears freezing on my cheeks.

"I'll run like the wind. They'll never catch me." She kissed the tip of one finger and then dabbed it onto my nose. "I will see you soon, baby sister." And then she was gone.

I wept silently. As I said, she was a terrible liar.

Her footsteps crunched in the virgin snow as she hurried away, and soon the sound was lost in the trees. I started to get very cold, and my little teeth began chattering.

I didn't hear the men approach. They must have been trained soldiers, because they moved quietly and without lights. The first I knew of them was when the log rocked gently, and I heard a soft crunch of snow. I stuffed two fingers into my mouth, terrified that the sound of my teeth chattering together would give me away.

There was conversation, but I cannot repeat it. They talked about what they would like to do if they caught a girl. I did not understand the words they used—I was very young and innocent, you must remember—but I could hear the gleeful cruelty in their hushed voices.

They sat only for a moment, catching their breath, and then they were gone. I could barely hear them go, walking as they were in the trail Anna had made through the snow.

Time passed. I did not hear any gunshots. At one point I thought I may have heard a scream, but it was very faint so I could not be sure.

Strange as it may seem, I think I slept.

Much later I heard somebody say my name. I tried to listen, but thinking was very hard. I think now that I must have been on the brink of freezing to death, because it was very difficult to focus on whoever was speaking to me.

"Come on," they were saying. "We have to get to Auntie's."

"I can't," I said miserably. "I'm stuck."

"You're not stuck, you're just cold." I was dimly aware of a figure standing in front of me, but the moon had sunk low and it was difficult to make out.

"Anna?" I mumbled.

"Of course," she replied. "I told you I'd come back."

A small spark of hope bloomed in my little mind, and I actually tried to move. The rotten wood was tight around me, but I could feel it loosening.

"Come on, we have to go." Anna turned and started to walk away, and I thought she was going to leave me again.

I found my strength. Wriggling like a worm, I got my arms free, and then it was easy to push the rest of me out. My joints were aching as I stood and looked around; nobody was there.

"This way, silly!" Anna's soft voice came from up the embankment, and I saw her silhouette. I stumbled through the snow towards her and asked for another piggyback.

"Not now, little one. You have to use your own feet."

The second part of my flight to Auntie's house was much harder. The snow seemed deeper and harder, and I had to walk the whole way myself. Soon my little legs were spent, and I sank to my knees in the snow.

"I know you're tired," said a gentle voice, "but you have to keep going."

Somehow, I jumped to my feet. "Slavka?" The moon had almost vanished and it was becoming very dark, but I could see her standing in the snow a short distance away. "I thought… the bad men…" I trailed off. I did not have the words.

"You are so close to Auntie's now," she said, her voice full of love and kindness. "Just a little further and you'll be there, and Auntie will make you a hot bowl of oats with dried apples."

With her encouragement, I somehow got to my feet and stumbled onward. I called out to Anna, but she did not reply, and neither did Slavka. Dimly, I wondered where they were, but most of my attention was focussed on the task of putting one foot in front of the other.

I had no idea where I was going, but I tried to walk in the direction I had last heard Anna's voice. I trudged for what seemed like hours, and then I heard a voice to my right.

"Wrong way," it said. I looked, and even though it was very dark, I could see someone walking away into the trees. They had long, curly hair, the color of steel in this dim light, but which would probably have been golden in daylight.

"Una?" I called.

She didn't turn, but simply said, "Follow me to Auntie's."

So I did. Like a ship following the beam of a lighthouse, I trudged miserably through that bitterly cold forest, following the beacon of Una's golden hair.

And then, just like that, I arrived. Amber lantern light spilled from a small window, and silhouetted against the greying pre-dawn sky I recognized the humped shape of Auntie's little cottage.

"We're here!" I cried happily, and turned to look for my sisters. In the golden light from the window, I could see them standing at the edge of the woods, all three of them holding hands.

"Come on!" I shouted. "Let's eat porridge!"

I realized that a fourth, taller figure was standing behind my sisters. I took a few steps closer, and saw that it was a woman. I did not know her, but she seemed familiar. Her kind eyes looked like Slavka's, and the corners of her mouth were crinkled with laughter lines, reminding me of Una. The protective way she put her arms around my sisters was uncannily like Anna.

She said nothing, but gave me one long, sad look before leading my sisters back into the forest.

From behind, I could see her hair. It was no color, not black, not blonde, not brown, not anything. It was beautiful.

\*\*\*

Nonno went silent, and I realized her story was over. Numbly, I reached for the pot to pour more tea, but found it empty. Without a word I rose and rinsed out the leaves, then refilled the kettle and put it back on the stove. I stood in silence while it came to the boil, and then made a fresh pot of tea.

I placed the tea on the table, then returned to the cabinet. Delicately, I set out three additional clean saucers, then set a cup in each one. Lifting the pot, I filled each cup in turn, and then Nonno's, and finally mine.

We drank our tea in silence. There was nothing more to say.

# I Share A Room With My Autistic Brother—He's Been Talking In His Sleep
## By Jacob Healey

---

1

A lot of autistic children are difficult to handle, but my brother Lucas isn't one of them. His 16 years on this earth have not inconvenienced my family in the least. In fact, I can say that of all the autistic kids I've met, Lucas is the sweetest and gentlest. I'm not just saying that because he's family; neighbors, teachers, and friends constantly note his calm disposition with surprise.

Until recently, he's never talked much. He spends hours on the phone with his best friend, an autistic classmate named Alex, and doesn't say anything but "Hi,

Alex," and "Bye, Alex." He's content to spend all day sitting in his banana chair and playing PlayStation. Getting him to leave his room for any reason is like pulling teeth—unless, of course, we lure him with Doritos and Nutter Butters.

He really is the greatest kid. That's why I'm so worried about him.

Over the past month, Lucas has talked more and more, but not while he's awake. It's pretty much business as usual during the daytime. At night, business has become very strange indeed. Though Lucas is a teenager, he's got the mental stature of a toddler. He says things a toddler would say, acts the way a toddler would act, and enjoys things that a toddler would enjoy.

My family has grown accustomed to this. If Lucas wants a peanut butter and jelly sandwich, he'll say "milk and sandwich" and we all know what he means. He does not speak in complete sentences, and he does not have a large vocabulary—which is why I've been so unnerved by the things he says in his sleep.

Lucas has never been a sleep-talker. I would know, I've shared a room with him his entire life. So when I awoke many nights ago to the sound of him babbling away from the bunk below mine, I paid attention.

The first thing I noticed was that his voice sounded different; my first thought was that somebody else was in our room. I almost would have preferred that. What I heard that night—and many nights since—was undoubtedly the voice of Lucas. But sharper, clearer, somehow more intelligent. Honestly, it's how I think his voice would sound if he were not autistic.

The second thing I noticed is what he said. "Hi, have we met?" Over and over again. Once every thirty seconds or so. It reminded me of something Lucas used to do in his childhood. He'd put in a movie, lie down next to the VCR and prop his feet up against it; then, he'd use his toes to rewind the most amusing scenes. Over and over again.

The third thing I noticed is how he said it. He wasn't just saying words, he was *meaning* them. The diction, the intonation—it sounded for all the world as though he were actually speaking to someone. "Hi," was bright and cheerful, the tone employed by perpetually happy people all over the world. Then, a pause. Hesitating. "Have we met?" Still upbeat, but with a hint of confusion. Maybe even trepidation.

I said Lucas' name, quietly at first, and then louder. He didn't respond. I hopped off the bed and used the light from my phone to look at him. He appeared to be both fully asleep and fully alert. He was lying down, yes, and his eyes were closed, but he somehow looked awake, attentive. He was on his back, flat as a board, his legs straight and his arms at his sides. His face pointed straight up toward the bunk board, his eyes dancing behind their lids and his mouth turned up in a small smile. I was about to go back to bed when his facial expression changed.

His smirk dissolved into a grimace. His face, once relaxed, was now scrunched and his eyes shut tight. He started to breathe more heavily, and I noticed a light shimmer of sweat beginning to appear on his forehead. I tried to shake him awake, but he wouldn't budge. His muscles looked so tense that I wondered if I should wake our parents. I decided against it, partly because I don't get along with our parents, and partly because I was getting freaked out and just wanted to sleep.

I scrambled back into bed a little too quickly for a 17-year-old guy. Just as I had relaxed and started to drift off, I heard Lucas' voice once more: this time a whisper, scared and helpless. "No. Please."

I couldn't get back to sleep that night.

Things were normal the next day. Lucas played video games, watched Teletubbies, and paced around our room. If anything was wrong, he didn't know it. I even interrupted Star Wars Battlefront II and asked him, "Luke, did you sleep good last night?" but he just nodded. "Yeah?" I said.

He replied with an affirmative, "Sleep good," his eyes never leaving the screen. Then he started making the whale noises from Finding Nemo. Like I said, things were normal.

I suppose I'm not sure how often he's talked in his sleep, but the next time it woke me up was a week later. It was loud. My parents sleep upstairs, so they didn't hear it, but they certainly would have if they were on our level.

He was crying.

"What are you? What do you want with me?" he asked through sobs. He sniffled, then louder, "What do you want?!" I hopped out of bed immediately and turned on the light. He was asleep, but his face was twisted even more grotesquely than it had been a week before. Tears rolled down his cheeks and soaked the pillow. I said his name forcefully, and even shook him, but he wouldn't wake.

I realized that rocky relationship aside, I needed to get my parents. I bolted out of my bedroom, then stopped in my tracks about halfway down the hall. Lucas was saying something new. I heard it more and more clearly as I retreated back into the room, overwhelmed by curiosity.

"Hello? Hello?! Oh, thank God." He sounded frightened for his life, and he was gasping, as though he were running from something. "I'm in trouble. My name is Anna Madsen, Annabeth Madsen, I need help. I need help."

My stomach dropped, because Annabeth Madsen is my girlfriend.

A brief pause, then, "There's a man, he's after me, someone, someone stopped him but I think he's following me, I hear him, I'm just running." Another pause, and a hysterical sob. "I'm, um, wait," Lucas continued, my girlfriend's words coming from his mouth. "The parking lot, the church, Baptist church, south of State Street, but wait, wait." I looked at Lucas in disbelief, too stunned to even worry about Anna. Lucas continued with, "I'm running, I'm already past the parking lot, oh, God, I don't know where he is, help, help!"

At this, I snapped back to reality. "Mom! Dad!" I roared. Louder. "MOM! DAD! HELP!"

"I think I can hear him still, it's too dark, I can't see him, I don't even know how I got here," Lucas sobbed, still lying flat and facing the bunk board, not moving a muscle.

My parents burst into the room, terrified looks on their faces. They looked at Lucas. "What in God's name —" my dad began, but was interrupted by more from Lucas.

"No, no, I am, I'm turning left! I'm—I can see Starbucks, and the gas station, and—no, no, I see him! I see his lights! Hey! HEYYYYY! HELP! HEYYYYY!" Lucas was now screaming at the top of his lungs. My mother was screaming too, trying to shake him awake. But then his face started to relax, and his voice at once became more relieved. "Oh, thank God, thank you, thank you," he sobbed. Then he was quiet.

That was everything he said, word for word. I'm able to remember it so exactly because the next morning, I listened to Anna's 911 call at the police station. The voice in the call was Anna's, but apart from that, I was listening to an echo.

When Lucas stopped talking that night, I dialed Anna with shaking hands. No answer. I sent her a text at 2:44, "Hey this is gonna sound weird but are you alright? Call me. Sorry. I'll explain."

I got this reply at 2:47, "Not really, I'll call give me a few minutes." 26 agonizing minutes later, my phone rang.

I listened to her story. A little after 2:00 in the morning she found herself in a hoodie and her pajama bottoms, barefoot, on an old dirt road near the industrial district (it's a small town, we still have a few unpaved streets). She didn't remember how she got there, but her feet were dirty, and she realized she must have walked. She knew where she was from the street signs, and found that she had her phone in the pocket of her hoodie. Panicking, she pulled it out to call someone—me, in fact—and she was struck, hard, in the back. She fell to the ground, scrambled to a sitting position, and turned her phone toward her attacker. He wore gym shorts and a hooded sweatshirt, and his face was too shadowed to see clearly. She tried to get up, and he grabbed her by the shoulders and threw her to the ground. They struggled for a few minutes, and she was badly beaten—the only shot she was able to get in was to viciously claw his leg with her long fingernails. Some of his skin and blood remained on her fingers when the police brought her in, the only evidence she was able to provide of her attacker.

Just as she was nearing collapse from exhaustion, another man emerged from the shadows. At first, she thought he was with her attacker, but her attacker recoiled when he saw the stranger. She said the attacker looked scared. The mystery man ran full speed at Annabeth's assailant, who promptly released her and took off. The mystery man caught up to her attacker about fifty feet away and tackled him to the ground. That's when she ran. She called the police, sprinting barefoot through the town until she saw the police officer pulling out of the gas station parking lot. She entered his custody bruised and bleeding, the soles of her feet practically torn to shreds.

At the end of Anna's story, she asked how I knew she was in trouble. I told her about Lucas. She gave the phone to the police officer, and I related what my brother had said to him as well. He asked me and my parents to come to the station in the morning and make a statement.

So, the next morning, my parents took both of us to the station. When we got there, there was a split-second when Lucas (who was completely normal when he woke up, albeit very tired) and Anna looked at each other. Their eyes met, locked on one another's, and as soon as the moment began, it was gone.

We made our statements, then asked the befuddled police officer, "Now what?"

"Now," he began, pausing as if wondering the same

thing himself, "uh, you can go." It sounded almost like a question.

I want to leave you with something Anna said to me later that same night. See, she was still needed at the station after I left, but she came to my place when they let her go. She looked awful. We talked about the police and whether they had a case. She said there wasn't much of her attacker's blood and skin left under her nails, but that they were sending what they could salvage to a lab for DNA testing. In the meantime, due to her lack of description there wasn't a lot they could do other than put the word out. You know, tell folks to be careful.

She said the police questioned her about her savior as well, but she could provide them with no helpful description. Her eyes hadn't seen much. Her mind, though, had a pretty good idea. "This is going to sound crazy," she said, "But I know who it was. I know who saved me."

All at once, the whole crazy situation came together for me. She didn't even need to say.

"It was Lucas."

2

So, back to my conversation with Anna, when she told me that she thought Lucas had saved her. As crazy as it sounded, and though I had no idea how, I agreed. Actually, given the circumstances, it seemed like a reasonably plausible explanation. Still, I asked her how she came to that conclusion.

"He looked at me in the police station, and he's never really even made eye contact with me before," she said, "but I felt this, like, sensation of being protected or something. I've actually been feeling it a lot lately, but it's hard to explain." She paused, shook her head, then said, "I want to see him."

She followed me into the bedroom, where Lucas was on the phone, silently listening to his friend Alex yammer away about God knows what. He didn't even look at us. Anna asked me who he was talking to, and after a bit of conversation, we pieced together that Alex was her cousin. "I had no idea they were friends," she said.

She crouched down by Lucas and tapped him on the shoulder. "Can I talk to Alex?" she asked him. With no hesitation, he smiled at her and handed over the phone. Anna and Alex talked for a while, and I sat on the floor next to Lucas. I whispered to him so Anna couldn't hear. I told him I didn't know what was going on, and that I was pretty sure he didn't either, but that if he had anything to do with Anna being alive, I just wanted to say thank you. He made the whale noises from Finding Nemo again.

Lucas slept a lot after the attack, but I didn't hear him talk in his sleep again until three nights later. I was downstairs, in our main room, talking to Anna on my phone. It was about 1:00 in the morning when I crept into our bedroom, whispering goodbye. "Goodnight, sweetie! Love you," came her reply. I stopped dead in my tracks.

Lucas had said it too.

"Wait, what the fuck? Did you—" I began, but she had already hung up. Trembling, I called her back. She picked up on the first ring. She and Lucas greeted me together.

"Are—are you ok?" I asked her, my voice shaking.

"Yeah," she and Lucas replied. "Why? Are *you* ok?"

My mind was reeling, and I couldn't gather my thoughts. "I, um—"

She interrupted. "Am I on speakerphone?"

"No, no," I said hastily. "That's, um, that's Lucas' voice. He's saying what you're saying. That's why I called you, uh, because last time that happened, you were in trouble, and—"

She made an *aww* noise, as if to indicate how sweet my concern was, then said, "No, I'm fine. Completely safe. In fact, I feel amazing. I think Lucas is looking out for me. Right now. Because I feel protected again, you know, how I told you that I feel like I'm being watched over? I felt it when Lucas came and saved me that night, I felt it when I looked at him at the police station, and I'm feeling it right now. I've even felt it when I've had bad dreams lately. It's nice."

A wave of relief crashed over me. "Good. Good," I

said, and looked over at Lucas gratefully. Just then, his facial expression began to sour. He gasped.

"Oh my God," he and Anna said in unison. "There's someone outside my house."

My heart dropped. "It's him, from that night," they said, voices trembling. "But he's… he can't get to me, he's trying but he can't." I asked them what they meant. "It's like he's walking against a wall," they replied. "He's on the sidewalk outside, I'm looking at him from my window, and he's taking steps in my direction, but he isn't getting any closer. I think something's stopping him."

A loud outburst from Lucas made me jump. "MOM! DAD!" I realized it was Anna, calling her parents. Through the phone, I heard them enter the room. "What? What is it?" A pause, then, "Oh my God."

"Do they see him?" I asked frantically through the phone. Anna said they did, and I silently thanked God that my girlfriend wasn't having a psychotic episode. I heard her dad calling the police and talking to the operator in a measured, authoritative tone.

"Yes, my name is Bruce Madsen. My daughter, Annabeth, was recently attacked by a man wearing a hooded sweatshirt and gym shorts. A man fitting that description is currently standing outside our house and, um, behaving erratically." A pause. "An upstairs bedroom, watching him from the window."

I listened to him direct his family away from the

window. "We're in the middle of the room now," he told the operator. He recited his address, thanked the operator, then said, "Please, hurry."

Lucas, still asleep, looked worried, and there were dark bags under his eyes. He'd looked more tired every day since this all started. "It's worse from over here," he said along with Anna.

"I wish we could see him."

I stayed on the phone, but things were relatively quiet for a few minutes. Then I heard Anna's mom say, "Someone's at the door." Bruce's phone rang. The operator, telling him the knock was a police officer and that it was safe to open the door.

That was the last eventful thing to happen that night. When the officer arrived, nobody was standing outside the house. A patrol searched the area, but found no trace of him. The police have started driving by the house periodically, and they've gotten the word out about suspicious activity in the neighborhood.

Much of their effort over the last couple of weeks, though, has been focused on Lucas. Several psychologists and other various specialists have come by the house to speak with him, each visit more unproductive than the last. And he's getting worse. Lots worse. He won't eat, won't speak, and the doctors say his body doesn't look like it's had a good night's sleep in weeks. They've been cramming him full of vitamins, and they'll probably have to start feeding him intravenously soon. All this, and nobody is any closer to figuring out what the hell is happening to him.

The nighttime episodes haven't stopped, either, but they're a lot more monotonous. I'll frequently hear him whisper one word, over and over, "Arian." I'm guessing on the spelling; that's just what it sounds like. But it's the strangest thing—on the one occasion I was actually looking at him while he said it, his lips didn't move. Like, at all. His mouth hung slightly open, and sound came out of it, but there was no motion in his tongue or jaw.

I suppose none of the sounds in "Arian" require much diction. But still, when I saw this happen, I had a mental image of a tiny man hiding in Lucas' lung, angling his head upwards, and whispering, the sound coming from inside Lucas, but not actually from him. The idea freaked me out enough to keep me from watching it again.

Meanwhile, Anna is nearly inconsolable. Her bruises have almost healed, and she can walk comfortably again, but she's out of her mind with fear. She has regular nightmares about being attacked. The man hasn't appeared in over two weeks now, which you'd think would ease her mind, but it actually seems to have the opposite effect. She gets more paranoid by the minute. She finds that the sicker Lucas gets, the less she finds herself "feeling protected."

She's also found herself in strange places, lately. "It's like I'm being hijacked," she said to me one day. Her kitchen, her backyard, her parents' bedroom; she'll go to sleep and wake up in one of these places, usually in the middle of the night, always with no recollection of how she got there.

Last night, she called me. "I'm scared," she said. Below me, Lucas was (thank God) silent as she spoke. She told me she didn't feel safe. She told me she wanted company. She asked me to come over and watch her. To make sure she didn't go anywhere, I guess.

I snuck out of the house, something I'm rather practiced at, and drove the 3.6 miles to Anna's. I didn't want my car door to wake her parents up, so I parked down the street. Bad idea. The moon seemed to cackle at me, barely illuminating my surroundings enough for every shadow to look like a man in a hoodie and gym shorts, staring at me from behind the trees and bushes I passed. After what seemed like an age, I reached her front door and she quietly let me in.

We usually only sneak around at night to, you know, have sex, but there was none of that this time. Mostly just me hugging her while she tried to calm down. But eventually, she fell asleep, and I lay awake next to her, watching the steady rise and fall of her chest. When she started talking, I was almost exasperated. *Not you too.*

Anna was mumbling something into her pillow, over and over. Over and over. I couldn't make it out until she turned onto her back. Then it came again, and it turned my blood to ice.

"Hi, have we met?"

Her body tensed. Her face contorted. It was just a bad dream. *Wasn't it?* The moonlight from the window gleamed off the beads of sweat forming on her brow. I tried to wake her, but to no avail. Her voice became small and frightened. "No," she whispered. "Please." I hoped to God that in a bedroom 3.6 miles away, Lucas had once again said the same thing.

I was just about to call for her parents when her face relaxed. I wiped the sweat from her forehead. She slept soundly, soundlessly, for the rest of the night. She barely moved a muscle.

Lucas protected Anna last night, of that I feel sure. From what? I can't imagine. But as I look at him right now, his bloodshot, exhausted eyes trained on the Teletubbies, I'm worried he won't be able to protect her for much longer.

3

I apologize for how disjointed this is about to feel; I'm just trying to figure out what's going on and don't have time to worry about making this sound pretty.

Before I get into that, though, I want to tell you about a loose theory of my own. As you can imagine, Anna and I have been brainstorming incessantly for any possible explanation, and we haven't come up with much. I mean, there's not a lot to come up with—at least, not within the realms of rational thought. But a little over a month ago, something happened in our family, and I'm starting to think it might be related to recent events.

My grandpa died of a heart attack. No need for condolences, he was a total asshole. Even worse, he was a religious asshole—the worst kind, in my opinion. For instance: he strongly disapproved of my relationship with Anna just because her family is Catholic. Ironically enough, Anna's an atheist; she just attends church to appease her parents. Now, it's one thing to disapprove of your grandson's girlfriend in silence, but it's another thing entirely to voice it like he did. Every time he saw her, he'd comment on how "immodestly" she was dressed, even if her outfit was perfectly appropriate. He frequently referred to her parents as "ingrates" and called Catholicism the "whore of the earth." He hated racial minorities (especially the Jews) as well, but that's neither here nor there.

Family is family, so a few Saturdays ago, I found myself dressed in black and delivering his wretched corpse to the dirt. My dad was directly in front of me when it came time to carry the casket, and he had a faint smile on his face. He always hated his father-in-law. Even my mom seemed to possess a vague sense of relief throughout the day. All in all, it was a surprisingly pleasant occasion for our family. Anna even came—she said it was to help us keep an eye on Lucas, who has a habit of wandering off when people aren't watching him, but I think she just wanted to see the old man drop six feet with the rest of us. Besides, she didn't seem to try overly hard to stop Lucas from sitting on every damn headstone he saw.

Lucas doesn't really have a social filter, so doing things that most people would find inappropriate or disrespectful, like sitting on graves, is almost second nature to him. Once, when he was six years old, his Sunday School teacher gave him a toy dog. At the time, Lucas was obsessed with "The Sandlot," and the dog the lady had brought him looked an awful lot like the dog from the movie. So rather than thanking this lady for the toy, like a non-autistic 6-year-old might do, he looks right at her and deliberately yells, "Oh, shit!" Just like Benny does when that dog jumps over the fence at him.

But I digress. I'm sorry to go off on a tangent like that, it's just that Lucas is doing worse. He barely gets out of bed, and I like remembering how he used to be. I guess the point of telling you all that was to say that my grandpa didn't like Lucas, either. He despised anything that didn't meet his definition of "normal." In fact, he seemed to think autism was just a phase that could be snapped out of. My dad usually hated my grandpa silently, but when the old man called Lucas a retard one day, I thought my dad was going to knock his fucking lights out.

Anyway, my theory is that this all has something to do

with my grandpa. I mean, he can't stand either Lucas or Anna, then he dies, and then all of a sudden crazy shit starts happening to both of them? That seems like too big of a coincidence to ignore. My theory isn't any more specific than that, unfortunately.

Still, we've tried what we could think of to try. For instance, we videotaped Anna in her sleep. She was initially resistant to the idea, but she gave in. After all, her nighttime excursions have increased in frequency, and she's obviously worried about it. So, two nights ago, we set up a video camera, "Paranormal Activity" style. She didn't like the feeling of being watched, or the glowing red dot that illuminated her otherwise dark room, but she was eventually able to fall asleep.

We watched the recording the next morning. And afternoon. Most of it was boring (watching someone sleep is even more dull than it sounds) but some crazy things did happen. These are the important things we saw:

• Anna dozed off while curled up on her side. Within fifteen minutes, she was lying flat as a board on her back, muscles tensed. "Hi, have we met?" repeated over and over. Then the whisper. "No. Please." But at the time this was happening, I was awake in my bedroom. If Lucas had spoken along with her, I'd have heard it.
• Whatever night terror Anna was having continued. She stayed tense for nearly half an hour, whispering the

following phrases at random: "Don't make me," "Faithful?!" and "He is not himself."

• Anna suddenly sat bolt upright in bed, eyes open and appearing fully conscious. She climbed out of bed, grabbed the chair from her desk, and placed it near her closet. She stood on the chair and reached into her closet, grabbing a small box from the top shelf. She pulled a pen and small piece of paper out of the box, wrote something on it, then put it back.

• Perhaps the strangest thing that happened took place not long after she wrote on the paper. She walked to the door of her bedroom, placed her hand on the knob, and pulled it open. But instead of walking out, she slowly turned her head toward the camera. She walked over to it, picked it up, and stared into the lens. Her eyes looked a little glazed, but she appeared to be fully conscious. "What is this?" she muttered. She turned it in every direction and examined it as though she'd never seen a camera before. This went on for about fifteen minutes. "Incredible," she said as she put it down. She walked to the door, pulled it shut, and retired to bed for the rest of the evening.

The following bullet points are some of our ideas and more information:

• Maybe Lucas wasn't speaking along with Anna's nightmare this time because he's getting weaker. That could also explain why the nightmare went on for longer. However, in light of yesterday's events with Alex, this is one of the more confusing aspects of the situation.

• Anna has absolutely no memory of getting up, writing on the paper, looking at the camera, or any of the other events of that night. However, she does have a vague memory of a recurring nightmare. She's somewhere outdoors. She can barely see a shadow off in the distance that looks exactly like a small tree. Then she realizes it's a man, and he's walking towards her. She isn't scared. He's in a colonial-style suit, and he looks nice. Handsome. He points at something, and she turns to look at it. When she turns back to him, something's different. He looks the same, but something feels different. Her sense of calm is replaced by a sudden and intense fear. Not very helpful, but unfortunately, that's all she can remember.

• I'm sure you're wondering what Anna wrote on that piece of paper. The words she wrote are mystifying, to be sure, but we're even more freaked out by how they were written. We paused the video, climbed up into her closet and grabbed the box. We looked inside, and there were 20 pieces of ripped up paper. Seven of them contained a single written word, thirteen blank. But none of the handwriting was hers. It was a neat, tiny scrawl that looked like it belonged to a boy. The indentation on the back of the paper suggested that the pen was pressed rather hard with the pen. We aren't sure which of the seven papers she wrote last night, but we took a picture of them. We have absolutely no idea what they mean or signify.

• We're most concerned by how she looked at that camera. Neither of us really believe in supernatural stuff, but it seemed like she had honestly never seen a camera before. Add that to the handwriting that wasn't hers, and we've kicked around the idea that maybe she's being possessed.

\*\*\*

Some of our theories in conversation have centered on the word "Arian" that Lucas said in his sleep, but we haven't made any progress on that. I suppose 'alien' and 'Aryan' are possibilities. I know there's a football player named Arian Foster, but somehow I doubt he's involved.

Our main theory has leaned toward Lucas' friend Alex being somehow involved. We were right.

Anna's his cousin, so she and I went over to his house yesterday to visit. Alex's mom answered the door, and invited us in for lunch. She said that she'd heard Lucas wasn't doing very well, so I told her everything that had been happening. By the end, her face was white.

"Alex used to talk in his sleep just like that all the time," she said. "Maybe he still does. The doctors said it wasn't an issue, so we moved him downstairs. It's the only way we could get any sleep."

She told us that for Alex, it all began when he was fourteen. He'd wake up in the middle of the night, voicing the panicked words of the unfortunate. It took his mother a couple of weeks to figure out the significance of what he was saying, but when she heard him sob that he didn't have any money, please don't kill him sir, she called a specialist. The doctors simply concluded that Alex suffered from chronic nightmares and that there was nothing to do but let them run their course. In the meantime, they said, it was probably best that his parents not sleep across the hall from him.

What the fuck, right?

Of course, we asked her if we could go talk to Alex. She told us his room was downstairs. We walked into the basement in silence, completely blown away by what she'd said. When we knocked on Alex's door, he opened it and looked at us. When he did, Anna gasped, and I felt her shift beside me. She was gaping at him with wide eyes and clutching her chest. I raised my eyebrows at her, but her attention was focused on Alex. "It's you," she said, her voice shaking. "You've been protecting me."

Alex turned around and walked into his room without a word. I grabbed Anna by the shoulders and whispered to her. "What are you talking about? I thought you said it was Lucas!" She just gave me a bewildered look

Alex turned around. "It is not Lucas," he said. Alex is autistic but very high-functioning, and his speech is usually disjointed, almost robotic. "I have protecting you from Lucas." We stared at him, blankly. He looked down sadly. "Not angry with him, please, Lucas, he is trying," he said. "He is not himself."

My stomach dropped. We had heard Anna use that exact phrase—several times—in her sleep the night before. I turned to her, and she looked absolutely horrified. "What's happening to me?" she asked Alex, pleadingly. "What are you protecting me from?"

Alex just shuddered and climbed in his bed. "I don't want to talk about it anymore." He gestured at the door. "Leave," he said simply, and pulled the covers over his face. We tried somewhat frantically to get more information out of him, but he wouldn't say another word. Communicating with the autistic is not always easy, unfortunately.

We went back to my house in a daze. In just a few sentences, Alex had turned everything we thought we knew about this upside down. We didn't know whether we could even trust Alex until we walked into Lucas' room. He was lying on his bed, half-conscious. The phone rested limply near his ear. He was listening to Alex.

We reached for the phone, but he grabbed it and pressed it firmly to the side of his head, shooting us a tired glance before turning over. Even the smallest movements seemed to require a great deal of effort. Anna knelt down next to him and pulled back the covers. He was only in a pair of boxers. "What are you doing?" I asked, but Anna only gasped and pointed. There, amidst the hair and freckles on his leg, were four long, pink scars—scratch marks.

"They couldn't find a match," she said breathlessly. I suddenly remembered the night of Anna's attack, and the blood and skin under her nails, courtesy of one well-placed swipe, shipped off to a lab.

"No, this is crazy," I said. "This is not right." My brain scrambled to make sense of this new development. "I watched him talking, in this bed, while you were—"

"We can't explain it," she said, tracing her fingers over Lucas' scars. "I did this, though. You know it."

I did.

"We have to hear this," she said, gesturing to the phone. We bolted into the main room and picked up the other line. I don't know what we expected—it was Alex's rushed, panicked voice repeating a single mantra, over and over:

"You are not yourself. You are not yourself. You are not yourself. You are not yourself. You are not yourself. You are not yourself. You are not yourself. You are not yourself. You are not yourself. You are not yourself. You are not yourself."

4

* * *

Now, it's time for me to step away and grieve—but first, I'll do my best to make it through this. I owe you that much.

By the end of yesterday, Lucas was hooked up to machines in our bedroom. He refused to go to the hospital —he hates unfamiliarity, and I think he just wanted his own bed. Anyway, the machines were making lots of noise, and it was obvious that anyone else sleeping in that room wouldn't sleep very well. That's how Anna, after some amount of begging, persuaded her parents to let me spend the night. But in all honesty, I think they really just wanted somebody to keep an eye on their little girl.

I failed.

As you might expect, Anna and I developed a nearly rabid obsession with solving this mystery. Our own safety and the safety of our loved ones were at sake; not to mention, the events were just morbidly interesting in their own right. But our parents, for some reason, didn't seem to want to hear much about it. I think they were probably trying to maintain some sense of sanity; wishing the whole situation would just go away. Of course, it didn't, and that's how I ended up at Anna's house last night.

The night didn't end at her house. Instead, I just returned from the police station, where I made a rather lengthy statement about the evening's events. I'm exhausted and anguished, but I'm writing to you now because the alternative is just sitting around, and that sounds awful.

Anna and I curled up together in bed, making small talk. Things just seemed wrong. We both felt as though we'd guzzled several energy drinks—our hearts beating nearly to our throats. We knew we weren't going to sleep. I kept thinking about Lucas, hooked up to all that miserable, beeping machinery. Around midnight, my phone suddenly vibrated from my parents texting me goodnight, and I jumped so bad I nearly pissed myself. I realized my bladder was painfully full, so despite Anna's protests, I excused myself to go to the bathroom.

I wonder how things might have been different if I hadn't left her.

I came back to a cool blast of air. The window, which was closed just a few minutes earlier, was now open. Anna was gone. I sprinted to the frame and stuck my head out. I saw her, running full speed down the street about two blocks away, wearing nothing but the panties and t-shirt I had left her in. I screamed her name at the top of my lungs just as she turned the corner and disappeared from view.

Almost instantaneously, it seemed, her parents burst in the room. I told them what had happened and we all clambered in her dad's car. Her mom dialed the police as we turned the corner Anna had turned—but she was nowhere to be seen.

We drove along the dark, empty streets at about twenty miles per hour, slowing down at intersections and peering down the crossroads, desperate for a glimpse of anything that might help us find Anna. Soon we were accompanied by two police cars.

The officers told us that they needed to keep track of us, and asked if we'd ride with them. Anna's parents went with one officer, I went with the other: a young guy named Officer Herron.

Herron drove through the streets with his brights on, and before long I found myself recounting all of the events of recent weeks. We must have talked for nearly ten minutes before we came to the edge of our town's enormous cemetery. I debated calling my parents to tell them to check on Lucas, but Herron's voice turned my attention toward other matters. "Oh shit, is that her?" he asked. I looked up. As we slowed, the squad car's headlights bathed the southern fence of the cemetery in an eerie glow, providing just enough light for us to see the girl climbing over it. Anna dropped gracelessly on the other side, clambered to her feet, and sprinted into the darkness. "She was attacked by somebody the last time this happened?" I nodded.

We parked the car on the side of the road as Herron put in a call for backup. He looked at me, gravely. He unholstered his weapon. "Wait in the car," he said, opening his door. I opened mine and followed him. He didn't stop me.

We climbed over the fence without hesitation, and

when we landed on the other side, Herron mumbled something into his radio. He pulled a flashlight from his belt and shone it in the direction Anna had run. It was a maze of headstones, and she was nowhere to be seen. Herron called out Anna's name as we stepped into the mass of graves, legions of the dead beneath our feet.

Herron held his gun and his flashlight together, frantically mowing his beam over the grass. Trees and larger headstones obscured most of our view. She could have been anywhere. I called out Anna's name, but Herron shushed me and turned his light off. "Jesus," he whispered. "Do you feel that?" I did. The moon gave just enough light to see the terror inside me reflected on his face. Something had suddenly begun to feel very, very wrong.

We stood in absolute silence until a faint scratching noise caused Herron to flick his light on and whirl around. Anna was about 100 meters away, kneeling at a grave, clawing frantically at the earth with her bare hands.

Herron and I looked at one another with dread. "Let's go get her," he said, and he sounded as though he'd rather be anywhere else in the world.

We approached Anna cautiously, our unease growing with every step. She made no notice of us when we reached her, nor when Herron's light illuminated the grave at which she knelt.

* * *

ARIAN CROWLEY
1794-1829
*A Faithful Servant*

The headstone was small, weathered, and half-covered by grass. Anna had begun to scratch it away, and in the light I could see her fingers bleeding heavily. One of her nails hung to the side on a flap of skin, almost completely detached.

The graves around me began to seem familiar. I looked around, and it didn't take me long to see my grandfather's modest headstone only two rows away. I remembered the funeral. I remembered Lucas, sitting on the graves. I remembered Anna, fruitlessly trying to drag him away. And that was when I realized that my dear departed grandfather, for all his flaws, didn't have much to do with this.

Sirens wailed in the distance, but we were too far in the cemetery to see the cars approaching the gates. Herron began speaking to Anna in gentle tones, then moved to put his arm around her. He recoiled sharply as they made contact, then swore as he examined something on his wrist. Anna was completely oblivious to our presence.

Herron shone his light up and down the nearby rows. "This is wrong," he said. "We shouldn't be here alone." He trained the beam on what looked to be a small tree in the distance, squinting at it, then shrieked as Anna knocked the flashlight out of his hands. He scrambled to it, picked it up and trained it on Anna, along with his pistol. She held her skinned fingers gingerly in front of her chest, looking frightened beyond belief. "What the fuck?!" he screamed at her.

"You shouldn't have done that, you shouldn't have put your light on him," she muttered, staring at the ground and beginning to sob. "You shouldn't have done that, he's not himself, he's not himself."

My heart dropped. Herron spun, his beam pointed toward the distant tree once more—but it was not a tree, it was a man, in a colonial-style suit, and he was walking calmly toward us. It was Lucas.

Well, kind of. This man looked older—about 30. Vibrant, healthy, and strong. Not autistic. Lucas' features were clear and dominant in his face, but there were also features from another face, from someone else altogether. His stride was familiar, and at once I realized where I'd seen it before. My mind flashed back to the man in the hooded sweatshirt outside Anna's house, taking steps toward the house yet going nowhere, impeded by an unseen barrier.

"Stop or I'll shoot!" Herron shrieked, and when the man continued on, Herron fired twice. Nothing happened. He looked at his weapon in hopeless confusion. The man, still approaching, was only fifty feet away from us. And then he stopped.

He looked around, almost as if he were sniffing for something. "Lucas!" I cried out, hoping to reach him. It was as though he didn't hear me.

"That's not Lucas," came Anna's feeble voice from behind me. I turned toward her, but her eyes were focused on the stone she'd been unearthing. "It's—"

"ARIAN!!" The voice rang out through the cemetery, angry and fierce. All at once, the approaching man seemed to shrink a bit. Lucas' features weren't as apparent in his face anymore. He was staring at us,—no, directly behind us—at Alex.

"Let him go," Alex ordered.

"Who is that? Where did he come from?" Herron demanded. Nobody answered him.

Alex walked briskly past us in the direction of the man who was somehow, apparently, unbelievably, Arian Crowley. Arian stumbled backwards. "You know this won't work," Alex said. "I won't let it happen. Let him go. Now."

Arian looked at Alex with a mixture of anguish and hatred. Lucas was all but gone from his face. "Fuck you!" he spat. But he was still retreating, still pedaling back from Alex, who seemed to grow larger and more intimidating with every step. "What does it matter?" Arian's tone became pleading. "He won't survive."

At that, Alex stopped and looked at the ground. "I know." Then he sprinted at Arian and tackled him, and

Arian didn't even bother to run, and they both disappeared as they fell.

The police backup arrived shortly thereafter to Anna, Officer Herron and I sitting on the ground near Arian Crowley's grave. "Those men," one officer said. "Where did they go?" We just shook our heads in a stunned silence, wondering the same thing ourselves.

About five minutes later, I had come back to my senses somewhat, and all I could think of were Arian's final words. "He won't survive." With a pit in my stomach, I called home, hoping that Lucas was alright but knowing he wasn't. My mother answered on the first ring, and she was already crying.

"I was just about to call you," she said. "He's gone. Lucas is gone."

# Miss Marni's Teahouse

# By Rona Vaselaar

––––––––––

"You're going to hell! Child of Satan, you'll burn in agony just like the Jews and towelheads! God will cast thee down! Down into Gehenna! Burn, witch!"

That's how I used to begin my morning. *Every* morning. I live in the same little townhouse that my mother lived in, and her mother before her, and for as long as I can remember we've lived next to Mrs. Thompson, who is the nastiest person I've ever met. Her voice has assaulted my ears since childhood—either she was yelling at my mother or antagonizing me while I played outside. I don't know how she came to the conclusion that we're witches, but no matter how kind we were to her, her words were always the same.

*Die. Burn in hell. Satan's spawn. Witches. Bitches.*

So, every morning, I'd walk to my car amid her screeching and try to tune it out as I prepared for the day.

After all, it's no good coming into work at a teahouse when you're stressed. *Your foul-mood will poison the tea.* At least, that's what my mother always told me.

Just like our home, the teahouse has been in my family for generations. It is always owned and managed by a woman, and we never take employees—they just aren't needed. Besides, it's hard to teach a newcomer the finer points of tea-making. Me? I've been studying tea since I was a child, as my mother passed down her secrets to me.

It's a wonderful job, a wonderful life, and I quite enjoy it. All except for Mrs. Thompson, of course.

\*\*\*

Every morning at the teahouse was the same.

I began by rinsing out the cast-iron teapot and teacups —you can't use soap on them, you know, and you can't wash the outside. You can only rinse them, and over time they'll take on the flavor of the teas you brew in them. Which is why I have a separate tea set for each kind of tea —Green, Black, Yellow, Oolong, White, and Herbal Infusions.

I'd set the metal teapots to brew hot water on the stove—you can't put cast-iron on the stove either. While prepping the water, I'd select the teas I would feature that day. Of course, a customer can come in and request any kind of tea they like, but I always like to give my own recommendations.

I would open the store at about nine o'clock in the morning and I'd spend the day serving tea. I had quite a few regular customers that enjoyed the healing properties of tea—people with stomach problems who liked the Jade Mint Oolong, people with anxiety who preferred the Chamomile Blossom, people who simply enjoyed the traditional taste and brewing process of Matcha.

Well, one morning, someone new came into the teahouse. Someone I never expected to see.

Jamie Thompson.

Mrs. Thompson's grandson, who spent most of his time caring for the aging crony, was standing at the front of my teahouse, watching me serve Mango Black tea to a few elderly tourists looking for something sweet and strong.

"Miss Marni. I see your teahouse is doing well," he began.

I noticed the elderly women staring at him in open appreciation—he was quite handsome, even I must admit —but I ignored him and went back to the tea preparation. Tea takes all of your attention, all of your heart; if you don't give it everything you've got, it will fail you, because you've already failed yourself.

Once the tea was prepared and the women were enjoying it iced, I stood up and approached the conspicuous newcomer.

"Mr. Thompson, I take it. What can I do for you today?" Most of the time, I'd start by asking what a customer likes, what a customer needs, what ailments are troubling them. I like to help people. But I was wary of Jamie. Nothing good comes from a poisoned plant.

"Well, I'm actually here to get something for my grandmother. See, her mind is… going. I read that tea is good for dementia, and I was wondering if you had any recommendations?"

It's true, studies have shown that certain kinds of tea are good at preserving brain mass, but as of yet, nothing in modern medicine is miraculous enough to reverse dementia. Still, nature works in funny ways. I went behind the front counter to examine my selection of green teas.

"You know, my grandmother, she probably wouldn't drink this if she knew you had prepared it."

I grunted in assent, none too keen on continuing our conversation. Jamie didn't seem to notice my reticence.

"But, you know, I'm hoping that maybe this will help patch things up between you. I think she'd really like you if she got to know you. I've always found you fascinating."

I selected some Gyokuro Imperial and turned to face him, appraising his expression. The light in his eyes told me that he was using his grandmother as a pretense to come see… me.

Oh. *Oh.*

Ignoring his obvious interest, I prepared the tealeaves

and rang up his purchase, explaining how they were best brewed and when to drink it for the best results. To his credit, he was very attentive, although he seemed more interested in my lips than the words coming out of them.

"Well, thank you for this. I'll give it to my grandmother and come back to tell you the results."

"You needn't bother," I retorted, anxious to get him out of my store. But he smiled in return, not a bit perturbed by my attitude.

"Oh, you can't get rid of me *that* easily, Miss Marni. I'll be back." With that, he turned and strode out of the store, the tourists still gawking at his tall, muscular frame.

That was the start of all the trouble.

\*\*\*

Jamie started coming in regularly, always asking for my recommendations, always claiming that my tea helped his grandmother *heal*. I sincerely doubted that, but I didn't bother correcting his ignorance. After all, it was just a façade.

At the close of each purchase, he would ask me the exact same question.

"So, do you have any plans for the night?"

Most of the time, I declined to answer.

I had to admit, he was patient. And persistent. He never missed a day. He was also sweet, in his own way. He handed out compliments like candy, but only ever to me. Sometimes, he brought in flowers, although I couldn't keep them in the store.

The scent would taint the tea.

He brought me sweets, on occasion. It was really getting on my nerves.

Finally, one day he didn't immediately ask me out. Instead, he presented me with an opportunity, one that was too good to pass up.

"Honestly, Marni, I'll do anything you want to just have one date. What do I have to do?"

"You can't afford a date with me," I assured, although the wheels in my head were already turning.

"Money isn't an object. Living next to my grandma all these years… you have to know my family is well off." He flashed me his patented, arrogant grin that somehow managed to hold a certain magnetic charm. "Name it, and I'll do it. I'll make you understand how serious I am."

He seemed serious. And I thought maybe—just *maybe* —he could be the one I'd been searching for. And if he was… oh, I'd never dared dream.

I grabbed out a post-it note and began scribbling the details on it as I told him what I wanted more than anything in the world.

"There is a tea grown in the Fujian Province of China called Da Hong Pao, or Big Red Robe. It grows so high on the mountains that only a few select tea masters are able to pick it. However, what many people don't know is that there are *two* strains of Da Hong Pao: the kind that is sold to the public, and a rarer kind that is used in medicine and religious rituals." I glanced into his eyes, but they remained impassive. I dared to finish, "I want you to get it for me."

He smirked, as though he was amused by my reticence. "No problem. Is it expensive?"

I paused to consider that question. "The tea itself… no. If you tell them you need it, if you tell them I need it, they'll give it to you. Only…"

"Only?"

"Only you have to fly to China and get it yourself. They won't send it to you, you won't be able to find a trace of them outside of their own little province. They're cut off from the world, and that's what makes their tea so special."

Jamie paused as if to consider this, making a very serious face and stroking his chin.

Finally, he winked at me.

"Consider it done."

My heart skipped a beat. All this time, searching for the right person, and he'd been right next to me, waiting for me to notice him.

Life seemed to move at a glacial pace after that. Jamie bought the tickets and set the date for six months after I gave him my request. During that half year, he studied Mandarin with a passion that I'd never seen in anyone else before. He also managed to track down a Fujianese native and began studying the dialect. He took very careful instruction from me as to how he could find these master tea pickers.

The day before he left, he came to see me, glowing with confidence as though he had already succeeded in his quest. I knew that the worst was yet to come for him, but he didn't seem concerned.

Before he walked out of my store, he stood in front of me and requested—no, *demanded*—a kiss for good luck. I was so excited and flustered, that I leaned forward and pecked him on the lips without stopping to think. He laughed at the blush suffusing my skin and walked out, anticipating grand adventure.

*** 

Weeks passed.

And yet not a word from Jamie. I tried to remind myself to be patient. After all, he had to arrive in China, hike to the mountains, and navigate his way to the secret property of the master pickers. Reaching them would take time, and that's not to mention gaining their trust. I could only hope that they would be a little more compliant when he mentioned my name.

And then a few more weeks. I noticed that Mrs. Thompson was too preoccupied to harass me—she seemed shaken by Jamie's absence. Not that it surprised me. He was, after all, her primary caretaker, and though she could still manage on her own at this point, she liked the company.

I was beginning to think that I would never hear back from Jamie when, one morning, I arrived at the teahouse to find a man sitting in front of the shop. He was an elderly Chinese man wearing traditional garb. In his arm he held a black lacquered chest.

My heart stopped.

When he saw me approach, he knelt in front of me and kowtowed three times. I inclined my head as a gesture of appreciation. Then, I opened the teahouse and let him inside.

We didn't exchange any words, although I am fluent in both Mandarin and Fujianese. Instead, I brewed him a cup of Golden Monkey Black tea, which he drank for ritual's sake. Once he finished his tea, he walked out the door and out of my life.

But he left behind the chest.

My hands shook as I lifted it, feeling its severe heft, and carried it to the back room.

Locking the door and closing the blinds, I opened the chest.

The first thing I saw were the bones.

Each and every bone in Jamie's body sat in the chest, neatly packed into a solid mass. I took them out one at a time, spreading them over my worktable, admiring their pristine white color. I had never seen something so beautiful.

Beneath the bones, separated by a wooden slot was the tea. The small, dark-green leaves with distinct golden flecks. That was how I knew they'd given me the right product. The flashes of gold were the ticket.

Yes, Jamie was the one that I'd been waiting for, the one I needed, the bargaining chip that got me my most precious treasure.

He was a perfect sacrifice.

*** 

Mrs. Thompson changed after Jamie was officially declared missing. It was assumed that he had died hiking in China —an inexperienced hiker can easily go missing without the proper guide—and, just like that, she found herself alone in the world. Her other children and grandchildren would have nothing to do with her. She stopped screaming at me in the mornings. She stopped coming outside at all.

But I couldn't just leave her alone like that.

One morning, I brought a special tea brew over just for her. When I knocked on the door, I half-expected her to cuss me, shouting obscenities and misquoted Bible verses.

Instead, she led me in to her kitchen. And I brewed

her tea.

I didn't say anything. I didn't have to. After a few minutes, she spoke on her own. About how Jamie had been so taken with me, sung my praises until she herself had begun to come around. About how much she had always loved him, how her whole life had revolved around him ever since he had been born.

She began crying at one point. In fact, she kept crying until I set her tea in front of her.

Almost absent-mindedly, she sipped the brew and gave me a surprised look. "This is good."

I smiled at her. "It is, isn't it?"

It only took a few days to get Mrs. Thompson to agree that I should be her new primary caretaker. Of course, she didn't need much care anymore, not after she began drinking my tea. After a few weeks, her forgetfulness, the signs of her dementia, they began to fade. She was as sharp as she'd always been.

Of course, that was intentional. I do, after all, want her to live a nice, long life, full of memories of Jamie and the agony of never knowing what happened to him.

It's amazing what a little tea and bone marrow can do to a person.

As for me? Well, I got what I wanted. I got the rare formula I need. I got the sacrifice for those brews that require something... darker. My mornings became much more peaceful without Mrs. Thompson's ranting and screaming.

Witch? Honey, that doesn't even begin to cover what I'm capable of.

# I Watched Video Footage of a Camping Trip That My Friends Never Actually Went On
## By Nina LaRocca

It was getting to be a tradition.

For the past two years we've gone on a camping trip together, me and my group of friends: Sean, Key, Sal, Monica, Gabe, Lin and her sister Lily. Monica's family is really wealthy and they own a lot of land out in Bumfuck, Michigan. We've wrapped up our past two summer vacations out there in the woods. We pitch a few tents in what's basically the backyard of Monica's grandmother's huge Victorian-style house and pretend we're roughin' it, when in actuality we just sleep out there for the five hours of the night that we don't spend drinking or playing video games inside. Cooking out over the bonfire and climbing trees is fun, but it's always only a small part of the trip.

None of us talked about it or admitted it out loud, not even Monica, but we were all a little afraid to be out there for too long. We had no concrete reason. No matter how many times the Pines' family assured us that the property was safe. I'd never seen or heard anything out of the ordinary out there—maybe it was just because I'd seen enough horror movies to develop a fear of the woods in general, but I don't know. Something about the air in the intimidatingly vast property just made me feel really vulnerable.

I got told just days before we were supposed to leave for this last trip that I wouldn't be able to take the time off for work. One of my fellow supervisors had to go in for emergency surgery on his knee and my store just didn't have the coverage. I was really bummed, but my friends didn't hold it against me—we all know being an adult sucks sometimes. I told them they could still use my cooler and my tents and camcorder, and that they should video-blog the trip for me. I hugged them all goodbye the morning they left and then I went off to my shift. I told Sal to call me once they got there because I knew he would be the only one who'd remember to check in.

Sal never called; none of them did. I left work at 10PM and tried to text and call all of them, but not one of them got back to me. I checked Twitter, Facebook—nothing from anybody. No updates since Gabe's "hitting the road" status from earlier that morning. I felt like throwing up. Something felt really wrong. Key's mother called me as soon as I started to panic and she sounded really rattled too—he hadn't talked to her all day, and he's really good about touching base with her when he takes trips. I'd later learn that that whole night, my friends' parents were all trying to get in touch with each other. None of them heard from their kids since they first got on the road. Monica's mom called the landline to the house several times. Grandma Pines was out of town this year, but Monica should have answered if they were there. She didn't.

Sean's father drove up to Pines' property the next morning with Monica's parents. He told me something felt off as soon as he stepped out of his car. When you pull up to the house, there's no fence or anything, so you can see if anything is set up in the area surrounding it. He would have been able to see if everyone had set up tents and gear as soon as he got up the path, but there was nothing. And he said all the house's windows were open and all the lights were on.

Within a half hour, they called the police.

I was asked to come in, watch the videos, and answer any questions I could. I've transcribed what I watched as best I could.

Clip 1, 10:45 9/16/2016

Gabe has the camera pointed at the rearview mirror.

Gabe: "How the fuck do you know when it's recording?"

Monica: "The green button is on, dipshit."

## Clip 2, 1:15 9/16/2016

Gabe is filming the back of Lin's car just ahead of them. He's talking to Sean and Monica but I can't tell what they're saying, even with the audio adjusted. It's raining really hard and I see flashes of lightning.

## Clip 3, 8:16 9/16/2016

A closeup of Monica. She's smoking and swinging in the rocking chair out on the back porch. She looks tipsy. She notices she's being filmed and winks at the camera. I think Sean laughs.

## Clip 4, 10:16 9/17/2016

I swallow hard when I see the timestamp—it doesn't make any sense. Saturday morning—Sean's father was already calling the police by then. I want to ask the cop what's going on, but he tells me to please just keep watching quietly.

Lily is flipping pancakes. She scrunches up her nose at the camera and Gabe chuckles.

Gabe: "You don't look so good, Lil. Didn't sleep?"

Lily: "How could I? All those fucking screams last night?"

Gabe: "The hell?"

Lily: "You didn't hear that shit? Lin and I were freaked the fuck out."

Gabe: "What the fuck? We didn't hear anything."

Lily: "Yeah, it fucking sounded like cats in heat, but— wrong. Like it wasn't natural."

Gabe: "We were out in the tents all night and we didn't hear shit."

Lily: "Lucky you! We came in the house at like four and it was still going. I don't know when it stopped but I guess I fell asleep at some point."

Gabe: "Did the girls say anything?"

Lily: "They're not up yet, I dunno. Here, can you pass me that—"

## Clip 5, 11:14 9/17/2016

A wide shot of the "backyard." I can hear glasses clinking and a couple of my friends taking drags of cigarettes. I see a figure standing far off by the edge of the woods, but whoever's filming doesn't seem to notice it. Then I hear Gabe's voice, followed by Sean's, then Key's; they're talking about the hottub needing repairs because the bubble jets don't work, and then the figure moves and Gabe sees it:

Gabe: "Whoa, whoa, what the fuck…"

Key: "What?"

Sean: "Dude."

Gabe: "Holy fuck, what the fuck, who the fuck is—"

Key: "Gabe."

Sean: "Yo, what the fuck, man?"

Gabe: "Did you see? Did you fucking see?"

The figure is contorting in the distance and I cover my mouth with my hand. It's shaped like a person, but it starts doing this odd twitching movement with its arms. They look almost like they're stretching out really long and then shrinking again. The legs are bending like a flamingo's. The boys behind the camera are yelling and freaking out. The shot cuts to the figure launching itself upward into the trees.

## Clip 6:

The timestamps are turned off.

It's night time, a shaky shot of the deck out back. The porch light is on and Lily and Key have their backs to the camera. They're crouched down sitting on the steps and Lily is sobbing. Key looks behind his shoulder and mouths "turn it off," but the camera's still recording. Key pecks the top of Lily's head and rubs her back but she barely moves.

Key: "Are you sure you saw…"

His voice is too quiet for me to hear everything he says. I'm pretty sure Gabe is the one filming again. I don't see Monica in the shot but I hear her voice, and then Sean's.

Monica: "What happened?"

Sean: "You didn't hear that shit?"

Monica: "What the fuck do you mean?"

Sean: "There's some shit in this fuckin' house, man."

Gabe: "Guys, guys."

Monica: "I looked in every single room, there's nothing in here."

Sean: "Freakin' the fuck out, man, I'm tired of this shit."

Monica: "Well what the fuck do you want us to do, Sean?"

Clip 7:

A shot of something—somebody—caught very high in a tree. Whoever's filming is panting and coughing like they started crying and it sounds like it could either be Gabe or Sal. The shot is focused on whatever's stuck up there and something breaks off the tree and falls. It makes no noise when it lands and that's where the shot cuts.

\* \* \*

Clip 8:

It's a shot of Monica's room, or what used to be her room when she was a little kid. I've only been in that room a couple of times—it's full of old childhood shit.

The window is open and a little breeze ripples through the curtain. There's a crash like glass shattering from what sounds like downstairs and I nearly jump out of my seat, shielding my eyes but the cop touches my arm. It's still just the room, pink and purple with sunshine coming through.

The clip ends with another loud crash and I swear I see flicker of someone's face, wide-eyed and gaunt, peeking into the corner of the window. Just for a second. I gasp out loud and whip around to look at the cop and he gives me this nod to keep watching.

Clip 9:

The last clip they show me is a blurred shot of a living room. The camera's facing the window overlooking the backyard and I can see a lit campfire. The TV isn't in the shot but I can hear the music to the menu screen of Mario Kart. The shot shifts in and out of focus and I can tell nobody is holding the camera. It's just been left on.

It was about a minute and a half of that, then suddenly the power in the house goes out with a crack and I shake in my seat. There's a strange, howling noise from the outside, but it's not a coyote, not an animal—it sounds like two or three people mocking wolves, but warped.

Something hits the window with a hard thud and I wince—there's blood spattered across it and through the smears, I can see somebody with oddly-shaped limbs standing by the fire. They don't move. They just stand there with their head bent down, fixated completely on the flames while the howling keeps going and I start to notice something. The howling sounds exactly the same every time—like it's a six-second sound clip playing on a loop. As soon as this clicks in my mind, it stops completely and I'm so thrown off that I almost don't see the figure disappear—it doesn't leave the shot, I don't see it move, it just vanishes. The fire goes out and the lights turn on in the house again. The menu music from Mario Kart is playing again and I can hear my friends laughing, the clink of beer bottles. The shot goes blurred and then shuts off.

*** 

That's all the footage they showed me. I was asked where I was during all this, why I didn't go on this trip, why my friends had some of my belongings, especially the camera. And I told them the truth. I told them about the previous two years, how nothing strange had ever happened on the Pines' property before.

I asked the police what happened to my friends.

They told me seven bodies were found on the property—none of them belonging to any one of my friends. Their parents were asked to identify the bodies and remains and none of them matched. My friends are missing.

I knew the cops weren't gonna tell me, so I asked Sean's father about the seven dead strangers. Were they people the Pines' knew? He didn't know. He just told me how he found them—six of them, in a clearing in the woods, laying in a circle surrounding a tree with their guts strung together, holding hands like in a prayer. The seventh body was perched up at the top of the tree, impaled through the head on the highest branch.

# Did Anyone Else Answer This Ad On Reddit?

## By SnollyGolly

---

1

My name is Matt. I haven't been sleeping much, lately. It all started a month or two ago when I lost my job.

It was a factory job, and a pretty sweet one at that. I got paid to pick aluminum siding up off one line, check it for defects, and move it to another line. I did that for 10 hours a day, and did a pretty good job.

The company got bought out, and they told us that robots could do our jobs just as well, and that was that. The company I'd worked at for 10 years just up and laid me off. I got a few weeks worth of pay as severance, so I guess that was okay. Unfortunately, I didn't really have any skills. Siding was the only thing I had ever done, and I wasn't really sure what I would do next. I got on with the job hunt and really tried hard. I thought for sure something would fall into my lap, but it just didn't. I started burning through my meager savings, and pretty soon, I was selling possessions to make ends meet.

Luckily, I just recently found a new job. It's even in my field of siding! I go out and install it on peoples' houses. It's really not that bad, just kind of rough in the summer. The crew I work with are really great guys, so shooting the shit with them makes up for the not-so-great pay and really demanding work. That's how I found out about Reddit. Tony and I were talking during a break a few weeks ago and he told me all about it:

"Yeah man, it's got all kinds of shit on there. Funny shit, sad shit, interesting shit, it's got all of it. Even naked ladies!"

Tony isn't a man of many words, but I could see his entire face light up when he talked about it. I figured anything that made Tony light up couldn't be all bad, so I signed up.

Reddit is really overwhelming. There's content everywhere. Baby pandas rolling down hills, candlelight vigils that make you tear up, and something called a "poop sock?" I don't know what that is, and I'm not sure I want to, Reddit is kind of weird sometimes.

Soon after I signed up, every spare minute was filled with Reddit, and I loved it. Well, until I saw that link. It was at the top of the page, and it said "Volunteers wanted! You'll be compensated fairly. Be your own person."

My paychecks hadn't arrived yet. I was barely scraping by, and after two weeks of eating nothing but ramen, I was sick of it. If there was even a slight chance I could make some extra money, I wanted to take it. The link went to a research group called "Gray and Dean Research." There's not a lot of information on their site, but from what I could find, they do some sort of behavior research. I looked around the site for a little bit to try and get a better idea of what it was they did, but the huge "sign up" button called to me like a moth toward a flame. They said I could be compensated for participating in their research study, and I didn't even need to leave the house. They were vague on the compensation, but I just didn't care. I think the sodium from all that ramen had started to affect my judgment, and I just took the leap and went for it.

They didn't even want that much information from me. They wanted my email address, and for me to answer a few questions.

"Do you consent to Gray and Dean Research monitoring you throughout the duration of the experiment?"

"Do you understand that Gray and Dean Research may withhold compensation until a time where the experiment's criteria is met?"

"Do you believe that you are your own person, and

that your actions are your own?"

Kind of weird questions, I know. You know in retrospect, I probably wouldn't have agreed to them on any other day. I was just so hungry, and poor, and tired of being poor. I thought participating in some harmless experiments from home would be worth it if I could change my situation. I also... well, this sounds crazy, so please just hear me out. I felt compelled to. I don't know that I can explain it, I just went to the site, and I felt like I needed to do it. Weirder yet, I didn't even really remember submitting it. I just woke up the next day with an email in my inbox:

Subject,

We're pleased to inform you that you've been accepted into our research study. A username and password has been created for you. Please login at the following address to start the experiment. We look forward to your participation.

Gray and Dean Research | Department of Acquisitions

~LINK~

Like I said, I don't really remember submitting the

form, but I was a little out of it. I clearly did. Flashing through my mind were images of me in a hot tub with models, on a private yacht somewhere drinking champaign, never wanting for anything else in life. These little daydreams were a welcome escape from my actual life, and with the money I'd get from this study, maybe I could at least drink beer at a lake.

I clicked the link provided at the end of the email, entered my username and password, and I was in the site. I'm not really sure what I expected, but this definitely wasn't it. I was instructed to focus intently on a movie that they would be playing in my browser. I was to watch it for a minute, and then answer a series of questions.

I read the instructions, and proceeded to the next step. I'm not sure what kind of video this was, but it wasn't like anything I had seen on Reddit before. It was red in the middle with a bunch of static around it. Something about it though, it made me feel different. As I'm writing this, I'm trying to find the words to explain how it made me feel, or why it felt slightly off, but I just can't. All I know is that the video wasn't right, and it made me feel disjointed and like I wasn't myself.

Even though every fiber of my being was saying this video was wrong, I watched the whole thing. I needed the money. After a minute, I was directed to the questionnaire, and that's really where things got weird. It wasn't that long, although I don't remember the exact length. Most of it was fairly mundane:

"Do you consider yourself a good person?"

*Well, yeah.* I think so. I clicked "Yes."

"Are good people capable of bad things?"

*Um, I guess so.* I clicked "Yes."

"Are you capable of bad things?"

I started to get a little uncomfortable. I had never really thought about what I was capable of. Come to think of it, most of my life had been spent sort of just drifting and being on auto-pilot. When I really started thinking though, I suppose I was capable of bad things, but I had no desire to act on them. I clicked "Yes."

"Would you hurt someone?"

This question seemed fairly vague. What did they mean? I played a little bit of football in high school, and I had given out my share of hard hits. It wasn't mean spirited though, it was just part of the game. I guess I could hurt someone though. I clicked "Yes."

"Would you kill someone?"

This strange little questionnaire was making me do more soul searching than I had done in my entire life. I was perfectly content not thinking about how far I'd go in unfortunate or desperate situations. I had to answer though, and when I really thought about it, I clicked "Yes."

"Would you kill someone?"

I just answered that! I was starting to get a little bit

freaked out now. I clicked "No."

"You are your own person."

That's not even a question. Of course I'm my own person. The strange thing about this one was that there weren't multiple choices, just a "Yes" box, so that's what I clicked.

After I had completed all the questions, I glanced up at the clock and realized two hours had passed. Man, it was already 11pm! *Where did the time go? I could have sworn that I started just 10 or 15 minutes ago. Also, when did I get such a splitting headache?* I decided to take a nice hot shower and retire for the evening to get some much needed sleep.

Honestly, though, I don't think I slept at all that night. I just laid awake in bed, and tried to let my exhausted body rest. My mind wasn't having it. A constant stream of intrusive thoughts kept me awake.

*Would I kill someone? Do I want to kill someone? Am I my own person?*

The disjointed thoughts kept racing through my head. I desperately wanted them to stop, but they just wouldn't. So I did something drastic. Something I try not to do; something bad.

I smoked some weed.

I know what you're saying: *Matt, you're working at a construction job and using tools that could hurt people, why are you doing drugs the night before you have to work?*

Well I used weed pretty heavily when I was younger,

and besides giving me a terminal case of the munchies, it typically helped my headaches, and always helped lull me to sleep. I figured half a joint might do the trick.

I had just lit it and taken a big puff when my cell phone lit up the night and startled me with its tinny rendition of Biz Markie's "Just A Friend."

I picked up. "Hello?"

I waited for a few moments, but there was nothing but the faint whispers of static on the other end, and then a robotic voice saying words I didn't understand the meaning of.

Then nothing.

Just like that part of my life had been erased, and I was here in the present.

I was suddenly in my living room during the day. My phone was nowhere to be seen. The light was pouring in from my window and illuminating my entire apartment. My mind started racing with anxious thoughts and panic. *Oh god, when did the sun come out? What time is it? I'm late to work! Why does my head hurt so much. Where is my phone? Oh god, I'm really late to work.*

Waking up late is the worst feeling in the world, but today, the splitting pain in my head was giving it a good run for its money. I trudged to the bedroom with squinting eyes, trying to block out the sunlight coming in from the windows to give my head some relief from the pain. My phone was lying on the floor and it said I had missed 7 calls.

"Shit."

I texted my boss and told him that I had been up all night sick, and lost track of time. I told him I'd stay home today, and be in tomorrow. He seemed to accept that, and I felt the smallest bit of my anxiety abated.

I sat down on the bed and put the phone on the nightstand. My head was still splitting, and I just wanted it to stop. I put my head in my hands and felt my eyes welling up with tears of frustration and pain, and that's when I noticed it.

Dirt. On my palms, and under my fingernails. Where did it come from? I had taken a shower before bed, and it definitely wasn't there last night. I don't remember weed doing this to me before. *Maybe it's gotten stronger?*

You know they talk about that on the news all the time. I pushed my confusion out of my thoughts for the time being. My brain couldn't handle it. I was confused and scared, but the pain center was overriding all logical thought. All I could do was lay down and try to sleep. I don't feel like I actually went to sleep, but then again, I don't really remember. I think I must have though, I remember dreaming about running through a field, chasing something, maybe someone. I don't know why I'm chasing it, or why it's running from me. I just know I need to catch it. Somehow during the chase, it falls, and I fall on top of it. There's a struggle. I hit it. I feel nothing.

So that's where I am now. The headache is starting to subside, but I still feel a bit out of sorts. I really just want to get back to sleeping regularly, and feeling like myself again, but I'm not sure how. I don't like how I feel. I don't feel like I'm my own person.

2

It's been an interesting couple of days I wanted to clear up a few things that I saw while skimming what I've so far written:

• I don't work for Gray and Dean research, and I don't think they are selling my information. I haven't gotten any other spam emails or phone calls, so I think it's safe to rule that out.

• I haven't gotten paid yet, but I hope that's coming soon.

Things have been going pretty well here, I can't complain too much. Although even as I write that, I realize it's a lie. It's just something people say, even when things aren't going well.

Let me try that again. Things aren't going well for me, and I think they're getting worse.

Things were looking up for a little while. My headache started to fade into a dull roar, and I was back at work bullshitting with Tony the next day.

"Hey Matt, what do you make of all this monkey talk on Reddit? People keep talking about taking their dicks out for that monkey that got shot at the zoo, but I don't see how that's gonna help fuck all," Tony said.

Listening to Tony talk about "that monkey" from the zoo made for a welcome distraction from all that weirdness last week. I tried my best to concentrate on doing a good job at work, and hopefully get paid soon. Unfortunately, when I talked to the boss about getting paid, he told me that the first check always took a little while, and I was probably at least 2 weeks away from seeing a dime. I left work kind of dejected, and the research study entered into my mind on the way home. I knew they mentioned compensation, but I hadn't seen a dime from that, either. I figured I'd follow up on it later and see if maybe they forgot to send the check.

That evening when I was back at my apartment enjoying another excellent cup-of-ramen while wishing it was Chipotle, my phone chirped. I had a new email:

Subject,

We'd first like to thank you for participating in our research study. Your experience and input will be immeasurably helpful. We'd like to remind you, that in order for you to be eligible for compensation, you must complete both experiments on our secure subject portal. Failure to complete both may result in disqualification.

Gray and Dean Research | Department of Acquisitions

~LINK~

Honestly, I didn't even really debate internally on if I should drop out or not. After all that weirdness last time with the headache and the missing time, I was certainly more than a little sketched out. The truth of the matter was though, I *needed* that money. I clicked the link in the email, and right away I was back at the secure subject portal.

I don't know if any of you have signed up, but there's something weird about that video. I dismissed it before, but after I watched it the second time, I was sure that there's something more to it. *How do they get it to look like sparks are coming out of the screen?* That's a really strange effect.

After the video, it was back to the weird questions.

"Have you ever been scared?"

*Well of course. Doesn't everyone get scared?* I clicked "Yes."

"Have you ever been really scared?"

I thought about it for a second and my mind went

back to being a kid and playing around with my friend, Todd, in the ditch behind my house. I was sure he would make that jump, but when he didn't, I was scared. When he was laying at the bottom of the ditch and not moving, I was really scared. He turned out fine, just a couple of broken bones, but the memory stayed with me. I clicked "Yes."

"Are you scared right now?"

It's the oddest thing, I wasn't until I read the question. Every fiber of my being was suddenly screaming at me. Yelling at me to jump to action, yelling at me to do something to get myself out of thie situation. I have struggled with anxiety throughout my life, and that's the thing with it. Your body tells you that you're scared, and tells you to run, but you don't know why you're running. I pushed the feeling down and clicked "No." Machismo, I guess.

"You should be."

Every single hair on my body stood up at once, and those voices telling me to run got even harder to push down. *What kind of joke was this?* Was this some bored scientist's way of being funny? I might have found humor in it before, but sitting alone in my apartment at night had me more freaked out than chuckling. I submitted the form and closed the laptop lid. I didn't want to deal with it anymore.

My head had started to hurt again, so I made my way

to the bedroom to try once more to get some sleep. I guess I hadn't mentioned it yet, but I've still been having a really hard time sleeping. I lay in bed and close my eyes, but I don't feel like I'm sleeping. Stranger yet, I feel like I'm dreaming. "How can you dream if you're not sleeping?" you might be asking yourself. I don't know, but it's the same dream every night.

I'm somewhere foreign—no idea of how I got there. Someone is whispering in my ear, but there's no one there. I don't even bother looking to see where the voice is coming from because I don't care. I can't hear the words, but I understand what they want. They want me to get "it." I don't even know what "it" is, but I start running at full speed trying to catch "it." It's pitch dark, and I can't see anything except silhouettes moving in the dark. I hear nothing except the labored breath of "it" as I gain ground. As I get close, I lunge at "it" and tackle "it" to the ground. My target lets out a groan as I make impact with "it." I hit "it" over and over, but feel nothing.

I gasp and open my eyes to find that it's morning, but I don't feel like I've slept even a minute. Rubbing my eyes, I try to get the will to get out of bed and get dressed. Thank god for Monster Energy, I don't think I'd be able to go to work without it. It doesn't really help the headaches, but then again, nothing really does. As I go about my morning routine, I catch my reflection in the mirror. *Man, I look like shit these days.*

Once I get to work, I can kind of get in the zone. It's really not that different from my other job. Pick up this piece, put it over here. Ironically enough, even though it's physically difficult, it calms my mind and makes me forget about the problems in my life. My phone starts playing the familiar rendition of "Just A Friend," and I start walking away from the job site so I can hear the other person. I answer it and say, "Hello?"

"Hello, this is a message from Gray and Dean Research. If you're expecting this call, please stay on the line; otherwise hang up."

I debate if I should hang up the phone right now. I'm at work after all, and if I thought money was tight before, it would be a lot tighter without a job. I figured it won't be that long though, so I stayed on the line. It was the same weird static and robotic voice I think. I mean, I don't really remember. I think it was spelling something out? Or asking me a question of some sort.

That brings us to today. I'm in a motel about 150 miles away, and I have no idea how I got here. My truck is outside, but I sure don't remember driving here. I've got 24 missed calls on my phone and 7 voicemails. I haven't listened to them yet, but I doubt they're good. I'm starting to get really scared now, it's not like me to lose track of time like this. I'm wondering if maybe I hit my head or something. *Would that explain the missing time?*

Maybe it's CO poisoning. I remember Tony telling me

about a story like that not too long ago. "Yeah man, dude was leaving notes for himself when he was all fucked up on that CO2 gas. Shit was wild, man."

I guess either of those would explain the headaches and the missing time. What I'm really having a hard time with though is the clothes. I'm wearing new ones and mine are in the bathtub. It's not that my clothes in the bathtub that worries me, it's that they are covered in blood. I know I can't remember what happened to me these last few days, but I checked myself, and I hope with all my heart it's not so, but I don't think it's my blood.

I don't know what's going on, but I'm terrified. I've never felt less like my own person.

3

It's been a crazy couple of days. When I woke up in the hotel room, I was really freaked. I'm still freaked, but I think I'm starting to understand what's going on. Unfortunately I sound like I'm crazy, and I'm even more scared than I was.

I went to the bathtub to look at the clothes again, just to make sure I had seen what I thought I had. They were definitely my clothes, and that was definitely blood. I've had chronic bloody noses since I was a kid, and I've ruined more than a few pillowcases in the night. There wasn't a doubt in my mind what this was. I'm sure you're thinking

"Matt, if you bleed in the night, is it so crazy that you ruined some clothes and put them in the bathtub?" No, it's really not that crazy in theory. The problem is how much blood there is. It seems like all my clothes are covered. I filled the bathtub with cold water—a trick my mother had taught me—and let my clothes soak while I dealt with my phone.

24 missed calls and 7 voicemails.

"Hey, Matt, this is Tony from work. You were acting all kinds of strange yesterday when you left. Did I do something to piss you the fuck off? Be easy brother, let me know you're okay."

I pressed delete.

"Matt, this is Bobby from work, you left mid-shift yesterday, and you're late for your shift today. I know you've been sick, but you gotta come to work, man.

"Shit" I say out loud in response to the message. Bobby was a great boss, and when I lost time and didn't show up the first time, he was understanding, but I suspected his patience had its limits. I pressed delete.

"Matt, you know I hate to do it, but I gotta let you go, man. If you get your shit together, give me a call and we'll talk about coming back."

Great, not only am I God-knows-where, but I'm jobless and have blood soaked clothes in the tub. If this wasn't me, I'd think it was hilarious, but in this very moment, I felt the weight of the world crushing my chest, and it felt like my head was competing to see who could give me the most pain. I wasn't sure who was winning.

I skimmed through the rest of the voicemails and missed calls, and deleted them all. It just didn't seem to matter. I figured I'd at least call back Tony and see if I could piece together what happened. I scrolled through my recent calls, and tapped his name to dial him.

"Jesus fuck, dude, you're alive," he said, sounding relieved.

"Yeah, man, at least for now." I replied, cringing from the effort talking on the phone required. "Hey, this is going to sound weird, but what happened yesterday?"

"Man, you don't remember? We were working and you picked up your phone to answered it. You walked away a little bit to take the call and then after a few seconds, you turned around, and started walking straight to your truck. You had this fucking deer-in-the-headlights look about you. When I asked what was up, you shoulder checked me hard enough to knock me down. That's not cool dude."

*I did all that?* I'd never hit Tony. For one, he was the closest thing I had to a real friend, and secondly, he's a big dude. Now he's telling me *I* knocked *him* down?

"Tony, I'm so sorry, I haven't been myself, lately. Ever since that research study I signed up for online, I've been feeling less and less like my own person"

"You gotta get some help, man, losing time like this

ain't healthy. I don't think I'd blame some weird website on it either, man. I signed up for that site you were talking about the other day, and it was weird, but it didn't make me into some kind of disappearing weirdo. Just get your shit together and call me if you need anything." He said.

"I will, Tony" I said and then hung up the phone. What the hell was going on here? I was in pain and confused, but I tried to push that out of my mind because it was time to get some answers. I collected myself for a minute and put together a game plan. First, deal with those fucking clothes. Second, head home and get some rest. Third, figure out what the hell is going on with me.

I went back into the bathroom, wrung out the somewhat less bloody clothes, and wrapped them in a hotel towel. "People steal these things all the time, I'm sure they won't miss one," I said out loud. Partially to alleviate the guilt my uncharacteristic petty theft made me feel, and probably also to put out my mind that I was trying to get rid of bloody clothes. I couldn't think about that right now. I needed to get home and figure out what was going on.

I took my soggy bundle of clothes to my truck, and hopped in. I opened up Google Maps and saw that I was a little over two hours away from my apartment. I turned on the truck, and started to drive. Now, I don't know if it's just me or not, but I've always felt at peace on the open road. Something about it calms and centers me. I started to think about my predicament. *Everything was going pretty well until this research study, but how does a website make me lose time?* It didn't make any sense. I didn't even spend that much time on the site. I just watched the weird video, answered some questions, gave them my phone number and got the... call. *The calls.*

That was it! Both times it was directly after that weird phone call. What did it even say? It spelled something out, and asked me if I was open? No, that can't be right.

Time had slipped away from me a little bit, because before I knew it, I was pulling into my apartment's parking lot. By habit alone, I got out of my truck, locked the doors, and walked to my mailbox to check it. Bills, bills, bills, spam, bills, a postcard, spam, bills.

The postcard was odd. I looked at it and saw that it was from Gray and Dean research. *Did I even give them my address?* Jeez, I must have. With all this missing time, I definitely couldn't rule that out. I looked at it closer. It was fairly plain on the front except for a picture of two smiling older men in lab coats. On the back, it said the following:

Gray and Dean want to congratulate you for your performance in phase 2 of our research study. Not everyone is cut out for the type of research we do, but you're one of the special chosen few. We will be making contact with you in the next couple of days. It's vitally important to keep this postcard on your person AT ALL TIMES. You will not be eligible for compensation if you do not. Thank you, we'll see you soon.

I felt a small weight lifted as I realized I'd finally be getting compensated. I can't say that all the hassle and headaches was worth it, but at least I was almost done. I folded the card in half and put it in my back pocket.

I walked up the stairs with the last bit of energy I had left, went straight to my bed, and fell down into it. It was comfortable, but every time I tried to clear my mind, my brain kept me awake with questions:

"What have you been doing with the lost time?"

"Where did all that blood come from?"

"Am I my own person?"

After realizing that sleep wasn't going to come for me, I opened my eyes and resolved to find answers. That's when I booted up the computer, went to Reddit, and searched around to get a clear picture of what happened so far.

That brings me to now. Have you ever Googled "Gray and Dean Research?" I'm sure some of you have, but I hadn't until right now. Nothing comes up. I mean sure, there are people named Gray or Dean, but none of them have a research institute together. I went back to their website to look to see if I missed anything the first time around. They claim to be based in New Mexico, but they don't list an address. *Maybe the phone number has some clues?* I decided to call it, and see if anyone answers.

"Gray and Dean Research is not accepting calls at this time, thank you."

Whoa, talk about timing, I just got an email from them. Here's what it says:

Subject,

Your compensation is on its way! As a reminder, if you don't have your postcard on you, you won't be eligible for compensation. You've come this far, make sure you get what you have coming to you.

Gray and Dean Research | Department of Acquisitions

Well at least that's good. Although I still don't know what I need a postcard to get a check in the mail. Does that seem strange?

\*\*\*

Hey, matt here again, i figured something out. Explanations for what's been going on! Last time i wrote, some weird stuff was going on. Probably had everyone really scared. Man that's nice of you guys to care. Except that it's really not that big of a deal. Got put on meds a few months back which effect my memory. Didn't remember to mention it until now. Real silly, matt! Entire time, it was just the drugs messing with my head and making me think silly things that aren't true. So my doctors have decided i should keep taking the medicine, but in a more controlled place. Except I need to go away somewhere so they can watch me. A nice place with lots of nice doctors. Really will be good to have so many people helping me. Caring people always make me feel better. Have a good time, and be your own person. i know i will!

• matt

# Something Happened 63 Years Ago

# By Jacob Healey

---

It's official: I'm an old man.

For the last couple years, I've comforted myself by saying I'm in my "early 70s," but math is simple and unforgiving. Today is my 75th birthday, and God, the years do fly.

I'm not here for your well wishes; this is hardly a milestone I'm excited about. I'm glad to still be here, of course, but I find I have less and less to live for with every passing year. My bones ache, my kids live far away, and the other side of my bed has been empty for just over eight months now. In fact, once I cast my vote against that goddamned Trump this November, I may have nothing to live for at all.

So spare me your "happy birthdays" and your

congratulations, if you please. I'm here because I have a story for you, and it's one I've never told before. I used to think I kept it inside because it was silly, or maybe because nobody would believe it. I've found, though, that the older you grow, the more exhausting it becomes to lie to yourself. If I'm being perfectly honest, I've never told anybody this story because it scares me almost to death.

But death seems friendlier than it used to, so listen close.

\*\*\*

The year was 1950; the setting a small town in Maine. I was a boy of nine, rather small for my age, with only one friend in the world to speak of—and his family, seemingly on a whim, decided to move 2,000 miles away. It was shaping up to be the worst summer of my life.

My pop wasn't around and my mom was a chore-whore—boy, was I proud of myself when I came up with that one—so I wasn't apt to hang around the house. With some hesitation, I decided the public library was the place to be that summer. The library's collection of books, particularly children's books, was meager to say the least. But within the walls of that miserly structure, I would find no undone chores, no nagging mother (God rest her soul), and perhaps most importantly, no other children with whom I would be expected to associate. I was the only kid with a low enough social status to spend his precious days of freedom sulking amid the bookshelves, and that was just fine with me.

The first half of my summer was even more dreadful than I had imagined it would be. I would sleep in until 10, do my chores, and then ride my bike to the library (and by bike, I mean rusty log of shit attached to a pair of wheels). Once there, I would split my time between unintentionally annoying the elderly patrons and deliberately doing so. One pleasant lady actually interrupted my incessant tongue-clicking to hiss a "shut the fuck up!" at me—the first time I ever heard a grownup use The F Word. Big fuckin' deal, I know, but in those days it was unheard of.

The dreary days turned to woeful weeks. I had actually begun praying for school to start again—until I discovered the basement. I could have sworn I'd roamed every inch of that library, but one day, in the far corner behind the foreign language collection I stumbled across a small wooden door I had never seen before. That was where it all began.

The door was windowless and made from oak that looked far older than the wall in which it rested. It had a knob of black metal that quite literally looked ancient—I wouldn't have been surprised to learn it was crafted in the 17th century. Engraved on the knob was what appeared to be a single footprint. I had the sense that whatever lay beyond this door was forbidden to me, and therefore probably the most interesting thing I would encounter all summer. I quickly glanced around to make sure nobody was watching me, then turned the heavy knob, slipped behind the door, and shut it.

There was nothing; only darkness. I took a couple of steps and then stopped, unnerved by the totality of the shadow which surrounded me. I waved my hands in front of me in an attempt to find a wall or a shelf or anything to hold on to. What I actually found was far more subtle—a small string, dangling from above—but far more useful. I grabbed it firmly and pulled it down.

Back in the day, lots of lightbulbs were operated with strings, and this was one of them. My surroundings were instantly illuminated. I was standing on a small, dusty platform that looked as though it hadn't seen life in quite some time. To my left was a crickety-ass spiral staircase, made of wood and appearing ready to collapse at any second. The bulb was the only source of light in the room, and it was feeble, so when I peered over the railing to see what lay below, the bottom of the staircase dissolved into the darkness.

I was beginning to feel scared. This place—wherever I was—seemed to have no business in a town library. It was as though I were in a completely different building. But no nine-year-old likes to let a mystery go unsolved. Looking back, I wish I could tell my prepubescent self to turn around, go back, do anything else besides descending that staircase. "You'll be spared a lot of sleepless nights," I'd say. But, of course, I didn't know that then—and I may not have listened even if I had. So instead of turning back, I took a deep breath, gripped the railing, and glared resolutely forward as I began my descent.

The wood on the railing was dry and covered with splinters. I immediately let go, holding my hands out for balance as I carefully traversed the staircase. It was (or at least seemed) very long, and with only the dim glow from the string-bulb far above me, my heart pounded mercilessly in the darkness. Even kids can sense when something isn't right, I think—they just don't always give a shit.

By the time my feet reached the cement floor at the bottom, the light from the bulb above was very nearly a memory. But there was a new light source, and God, I'll never forget it. Directly in front of me was a door: massive, and a deep shade of red. The light was coming from behind the door, and it shone out in thin lines from all four sides—a sinister, dimly glowing rectangle. For the second time, I took a deep breath and went through a door I shouldn't have.

In contrast to the dank room I entered from, the room behind the door was blinding. When my eyes adjusted, what I saw nearly took my breath away.

It was a library. The most perfect library imaginable.

I gaped in wonder as I stepped, almost reverently,

further into the room. It was beautiful. It was smaller than the library above, much smaller, but it seemed to be almost tailor-made for me. The shelves were packed with brightly colored titles, both armchairs in the middle of the room were exquisitely comfortable, and the smell—my God, the smell—was simply unbelievable. Sort of a mixture of citrus and pine. I simply can't do it justice with words, so I'll suffice it to say that I've never smelled anything better. Not in my 75 years.

*What was this room? Why had I never heard of it before? Why was nobody else here?* Those were the questions I should have been asking. But I was intoxicated. As I gazed around at all the books and basked in the smell of paradise, I could only form one thought: *I will never be bored again.*

*\*\*\**

In truth, boredom only hid from me for three years. It was on my 12th birthday, 63 years ago to this day, that everything changed.

Before that day, I visited my basement sanctuary as often as I could—usually several times a week. I never saw another soul down there, yet strangely remained free of suspicion. I never removed a book from that room, but instead would pick up a particular volume wherever I had stopped reading during my previous visit. I sat, always in the same deep purple armchair, and always leaving its twin barren and directly across from myself. That armchair was mine, the other was—well, I suppose I couldn't have articulated it then much better than I can now. But it wasn't mine, that's for damn sure.

On my twelfth birthday, I arrived later than usual. My mom had invited a couple classmates and some cousins over to our house to celebrate, a gesture which I found more tedious than touching—really, I just wanted to spend my birthday sitting and reading and smelling paradise. Eventually, our guests went home, and I made it to the library about fifteen minutes before closing time. That didn't matter; the workers never checked down there before they locked up. I was free to stay as late as I wished. This particular night, I was devouring the final chapters of an epic adventure; knights, swords, dragons, and the like. I didn't smell it until I read the final words and closed the book.

The once exquisite aroma of that room had turned sour. I sat for a moment, unsettled. Objectively, I could recognize that the smell was actually the same as it had been before—that mixture of citrus and pine. I just perceived it differently, and I didn't like it anymore. It was the nasal version of an optical illusion; you know, the one that looks like a young woman glancing backward, but all of a sudden you see that it's really an old woman facing toward you? You can't unsee that, and I couldn't unsmell this. The spell was broken.

The odor also seemed, for the first time, to be coming from somewhere specific. With a fair amount of trepidation, I stalked around the room, sniffing the air like a crazed canine until I came to a shelf near the back. The shelf was perfectly normal, with the exception of one title —a large, leatherbound cover of solid faded maroon, with one striking black footprint at the top of the spine. This was the source of the smell. I opened the front cover, and saw one sentence scrawled neatly in blood-red ink atop the first page:

*Rest your sorrows down, friend, and leave them where they lie.*

I stared at this sentence, mesmerized, as I began to retreat to my chair. I turned a page. Blank. The smell became stronger. Another page, blank, and the smell grew stronger still. I stopped for a moment, suppressed a gag, and continued walking. Then, as I neared the armchairs, I turned one final page—and there, in the same sinister print, was the last thing I expected to see: my own name. I dropped the book. I began to sprint toward the door, but as I shifted my gaze forward, my heart leapt to my throat and I stopped in my tracks.

The empty chair wasn't empty anymore.

An aged man in a suit sat before me, one leg crossed over the other, contemplating me with piercing gray eyes and a light smirk. This was all too much. I fell to my knees and expelled the contents of my stomach onto the carpet. I wiped my mouth, staring at my vomit, when I heard the man let out a chuckle.

I stared at him disbelievingly. "Who are you?" I asked, panic in my voice.

The man leapt to his feet, grabbed me gently by the shoulders, and helped me to my chair. He sat, once again, in his own chair. The chair that belonged to someone else. "I fear we got off to a bad start," he said, glancing at the pile of sick on the carpet. "The smell... it does take some getting used to."

"Who are you?" I repeated.

"Tonight, you will know hardship like you've never before known," he said. "I come as a friend, offering you refuge from it, and from all other storms which lie ahead."

I wanted nothing more than to leave at that moment, but I remained seated. I asked him what he was talking about.

"Your mother is dead, my boy. By her own hand, in her kitchen. The scene is gruesome, I must admit," he said in sorrowful tones, but was there a playful glint in his eye? "Surely you wish to avoid this path. I can show you a safer one."

My blood ran cold at the horrors this man spoke of, but I did not believe him. "What do you want with me?" I demanded, trying to sound braver than I felt. He laughed, an old, raspy yelp that seemed to shake him to his bones.

"Nothing but your friendship, dear boy," he said. Then, sensing I found his answer inadequate, he expounded. "I want you to come on a journey with me. My work is noble and you will make a fine apprentice. And maybe, when I'm done," he sighed tiredly, running his bony fingers through his thin white hair, "maybe then, my work can be yours."

I stood up, shuffling toward the door but never breaking his gaze. "You're crazy," I told him. "My mom. She's not."

"See for yourself, if you must," he said, gesturing toward the door. I threw him a contemptuous glare and bolted for the exit. As my hand closed around the knob, he said my name softly. In spite of myself, I turned around.

"Your road won't be easy, friend. If it ever becomes too much for you, and I mean ever," he said, pausing to sweep his hand over the room, "you know where to find me."

I slammed the door behind me and took the decrepit stairs two at a time. I exited the library, clambered onto my bike, and high-tailed it home. The front door was wide open. I dismounted, leaving my bike in a heap on the ground, and approached the house cautiously. The old man was lying—he must have been. Still, tears began to sting my eyes. Heart pounding, I stepped inside and called for my mother. I heard no answer, so I turned into the kitchen.

To this day, I don't know why she did it.

* * *

***

I've lived in that small town in Maine my entire life, although I've kept mostly clear of the public library. Once, in my late 20s, I summoned the courage to step inside. Life was good at that time, and my fear had begun to morph into idle curiosity. Where the door to my basement sanctuary once stood was only a blank wall. I asked the librarian what had become of that basement, though in my heart I knew the answer. There was no basement, she said. There had never been a basement. In fact, if she had her facts correctly, city zoning ordinances prohibited a basement in the area.

I've been haunted by that sickly-sweet smell, that poisonous blend of citrus and pine, ever since that long ago birthday. When I saw my mother in the kitchen that day, collapsed in a pool of her own blood, I smelled it. When a man claiming to be my father knocked on my college apartment door, begged me for money and beat me to within an inch of my life when I refused, I smelled it. When my wife miscarried our second child, I smelled it, and again when she miscarried our fourth. When our oldest son got behind the wheel of the family Buick completely shitfaced and got his girlfriend killed, I smelled it.

I began to smell it periodically as my wife became sick.

She died late last year, and now, I'm alone for the first time in more than half a century. Now, I smell it every day, and it feels like an invitation.

A few months ago, I went back to the library and the small oak door with the ancient handle was there—right where it used to be. My evening walk has brought me past that library every day since, but I haven't gone inside. Maybe tonight I will. I'm frightened to die, yes, but lately I'm even more frightened to keep living. The old man was right—my road hasn't been easy, and I doubt it will get any easier.

*Rest your sorrows down, friend, and leave them where they lie.*

He promised relief. A refuge, he said. *Was he right about that too?* There's only one way to find out. After all, I still know where to find him.

# There Are People Outside My Windows During Blackouts

# By Nick Botic

———————

1

I feel bad for my child—she was the first one to experience the terror my wife and I would soon feel for ourselves. It began about a week ago, and I don't know what to do.

Me, my wife, Kimmy, and our 6-year-old daughter Anna live in a modest 4 bedroom house, in a place where we are victim to semi-regular blackouts. Only lasting for a minute or two most of the time, they are more of a minor inconvenience than a true problem. We've been dealing with them for close to three years now, and have learned to live with them. On the plus side, being subject to somewhat frequent power outages has afforded us a

145

relatively cheap mortgage.

That's neither here nor there. As I said, this began about a week ago. Anna came into our bedroom at about 1:30 in the morning and nudged me awake. I had to look at my phone to see the time, because the clock on my nightstand read a steadily blinking 12:00. We must have had a blackout.

"What's wrong sweetie?" I asked, my comforting tone thankfully overpowering the irritation in my voice due to being woken up.

"There's a man outside and he won't stop looking in my window."

My heart sank into my stomach, and I jumped out of bed, telling my daughter to stay with mommy. I grabbed a baseball bat and ran to her room, looking out both her windows, and I could see no one. I did a circle around my house in both directions, looking into the distance every which way, and saw nothing out of the ordinary. Just other houses on our block, our backyard as quiet as it could be, and the woods past our fence as peaceful as they ever were.

Convinced my daughter had just had a bad dream, I told her I checked and no one was there, and that she could stay in bed with us that night. The following morning, she asked about the "man outside her window" again. I told her that she had just had a bad dream and to not worry about it.

That night, I was up late, getting some writing done (my profession), when the power once again went out. My laptop switched to battery mode, so I kept working. It was about a minute and a half later when the power came back on and I heard footsteps coming down our hardwood hallway floor. As I turned around, I saw my daughter stumble into my office, with a look of sheer horror in her eyes. She said that the same man and two other people had come up to her window, and said that they "were gonna get you and mommy and save me for last."

Through her hysteric tears, she was hardly intelligible. I once again ran around the house, searching for anything that could confirm my daughter's reason for being so horrified. I found nothing, and again let her sleep in our bed, while I eventually dozed off in my office. I was awoken in the morning by my wife, who had been unaware of the events the night prior. I told her I had checked it out, and we had nothing to fear. She wasn't satisfied, and resolved to sleep in Anna's room with her that night.

I was once again working on my project late when the power once again went out. Now, when I say we get semi-regular blackouts, I mean maybe three or four times a week, maybe, and like I said, only for a minute or two at a time each. Rarely did we get two in a row, and I don't think we ever had a blackout three nights in a row. This one lasted much shorter than the rest. It lasted about 15 seconds, and about three seconds before the power returned, I heard my wife let out a shrill scream. I sprinted out of my office and into Anna's room as her nightlight and alarm clock came back on, and found my wife and daughter huddled in the corner of the room. I asked what was wrong, and my wife confirmed Anna's stories. This time, five people had come up to the window, and had been smiling and waving, but not in a nice way. Kimmy said their smiles were crooked and wide, as if they were straining to smile as big as they could, with their eyes wide open.

My only response to being told this was, "What the fuck?" She said when the lights came back on, she looked away for a moment, and when she looked back, the people were gone. We called the police and made a statement, and they agreed to put a patrol car down the street from our house and have an officer keep an eye on us. This gave us a sense of peace, if only for that night.

We rested easy for most of the night, Anna sleeping in the bed with my wife in our room, and I was in the living room watching TV. Until the power went out. I looked out the window and to my surprise, the rest of the houses on the block were still with power. Porch lights were still on, and the glow of televisions in other houses still illuminated through their windows. It was then that I saw a group of people slowly walking down the street towards our house. They were in the middle of the street, under the still shining street lights, just casually strolling, and the cop was doing nothing.

As the people got closer, I noticed they were walking very loosely, their bodies being held up with the least amount of effort possible, their backs arched backwards a tiny bit, with their arms flailing back and forth as their nimble legs carried them toward my home. And it was when they got even closer that I saw their smiles. My wife hadn't exaggerated; even from a distance, the street lights showed me that their neck veins were popping out from straining to smile as wide as they could. I stared out my window at them, trying to figure out what they were doing, when from out of nowhere, one of them popped up in front of me, sending me falling back onto the floor.

It was a man, looking to be about 30, just standing there, waving at me with that gross smile stretching his face. I stood up and looked out the window I could see the cop through. Not only was he sitting there doing nothing, but there was another group of three of these—whatever they are—flailing past his car. Unless he was sleeping, there is no way he could have missed them. They all converged on the sidewalk adjacent to my front yard, and lined up horizontally. Then, as if in a choreographed fashion, from the left to the right, each one began doing their creepy walk towards my house.

I was frozen in fear for a moment, but then snapped out of it. I had to make sure my family was okay, so I rushed down the hall to my bedroom. To my horror, my wife and daughter were not in the bed where I'd left them earlier. There was however, two of these freaks outside each of our bedroom windows. I screamed at the top of my lungs "What the fuck did you do with my family?!" And just then, the lights turned back on, and my wife and daughter came out of our walk-in closet. They both hugged me and cried, while I stood there in shock.

I looked out the window and saw no one. I broke away from the hug and rushed back to the living room. There was no one in any direction for as far as the eye could see. I couldn't make sense of this. I armed myself with my baseball bat and walked over to the police car. There he was, wide awake, sitting and listening to music. I asked what the hell he was doing there if he wasn't gonna do anything to help us. I explained that people had walked directly towards him and past him, and he just sat there doing nothing. He claimed he hadn't seen anyone, and had been awake the whole time. He then told me to get back in my house while he went and did a search of the neighborhood. I saw him drive off down the street, shining his spotlight through each and every yard and side yard on the block. My family and I stayed up together in the living room for the rest of the night.

Nothing happened for the next two nights, so we thought that whatever was going on had passed. Even so, I went to my father's house the day after the last incident and retrieved the gun I had there: a Glock 37. Normally, my wife didn't allow guns in the house, but with the events of the previous few nights, she made an exception to the rule for as long as we had to deal with this. It was last night that things happened again.

The three of us had taken to sleeping in the living room together so as to stay together and to be the most prepared if something happened again. We were all asleep when I was awoken by a tapping on the window. The first thing I noticed was all the power was out, and I took a quick glance across the street to see the neighbor's porch light still on. It was once again only us that had been affected by this power outage. I then redirected my attention to the direction of the tapping.

Once I looked, the person in the window stopped tapping, and all the while with that disgusting grin, waved to me, as if it was pleased I'd noticed it. I grabbed the gun and showed it to the prowler, but it didn't phase her at all. She just kept right on waving and smiling. I then noticed that there was a large group, between 10 and 15 of these things, lackadaisically flailing down the street. I looked out the other window; an equally large group was coming from the other direction. I knew one thing, and that was I didn't have enough bullets for all these people. They again converged by lining up in front of my house, then they all started waving. Every single one of them.

It stayed this way for about 10 seconds before one in the middle stopped waving and began moving forward. It was doing its loose walk, though this time much more slowly, up the walkway to my door. I ran to the door and told my family, now awake, to stay down and cover their eyes and ears. They heeded the order as I put both hands on the Glock. My plan was to wait until the man got to the door, knowing I'd hear him come up the creaky wooden steps to my porch, and then swing my door open and find, at gunpoint, what he wanted with me and my family.

Sure enough, I heard the creaking of the steps as he surely bounced up each one of the three leading up to my porch. His scraping footsteps got closer and my heart beat raised. I had never done anything like this before and I truly felt like I wasn't prepared to put a gun in someone's face. The will to protect my family won out, and as our doorknob rattled from whoever it was outside attempting to get into my house, I swung the door open. As if it was planned, the very moment the door opened, the lights went back on. There was no one there. No one in the street, no one at our living room window, no one lined up in the front yard. It was as if they'd vanished into thin air. I told my family we were okay, if only for that night.

It's the afternoon now, and my wife and daughter have gone to a hotel about 5 minutes away from our house. I made sure they got a room on a higher floor than the first, and politely asked hotel security to keep an extra keen eye on the grounds that night, especially in the case of any blackouts. I've decided to stay at home tonight, so I can do whatever I can to figure out what it is I'm dealing with and what they want.

Wish me luck.

2

I snapped out of my nerve-induced show of resilience and false machoism and decided to go back to the hotel. From my neighborhood, I can essentially take side streets the entire way to the back of the hotel, with the main street being on the other side of the main building. As I drove down the street, each street light I passed went out. One by one.

The darkness behind me seemed to envelope everything else, even the moonlight. I sped up, but the darkness caught up to me. I began seeing people walking from the sidewalk towards the middle of the street in that horrible, albeit ridiculous, flail. Whatever was going on was not limited to my house.

These things walked in the street and waved as I drove by, dodging me as I swerved around them.

I finally made it to the hotel and went up to the fourth floor to reunite with my family with some of the high-powered flashlights that I had out in the garage back home. My wife answered the door, and I saw my daughter passed out on the large lounge chair. I told my wife I had seen the things, which our daughter had started to call "smilers," on the street on my way to the hotel. My wife reported back to me that nothing of concern had happened at the hotel. This gave me a well-needed sense of peace, as I was starting to feel suffocated by fear and paranoia.

My wife and I fell asleep on the couch, our daughter in the chair to our left. I was awoken by a tapping sound coming from the proper bedroom around 3 AM. Upon opening my eyes I knew there had been a blackout. I quickly darted up and grabbed a flashlight and headed into the room. I shined the flashlight in the room, and when it was clear, I walked towards the drawn blinds. The only thing I could think of was how someone was knocking on a fourth floor window where there was no balcony.

I quickly opened the blinds to an empty window. I breathed a sigh of relief, but perked back up when I heard my wife loudly whisper my name. I rushed back to the living room and saw movement in the crack between the curtains on the door to the balcony. I told my daughter to cover her eyes and approached the window.

I kept the flashlight pointed forward as I inched towards the covered sliding glass door. When I reached it, I flung the curtains open and shined the light forward, directly on the three grinning individuals that stood before me. It didn't seem to affect them at all. They just stood there, dirty, their hair ratty and knotted up with junk in the corners of their mouths. Their clothes were tattered and torn, with dirt stains all over the place. Their teeth were unkept, for the ones that even had all their teeth.

The main thing I noticed was their eyes. Through all of the filth, each and every one of their eyes shone bright in the reflection of the flashlight. I don't know how I hadn't noticed it before. Surely their eyes glistened in the dark. They were mesmerizing. I found myself just standing there, looking into one of their eyes when my wife spoke my name in the same tone. I snapped out of it.

I asked, loudly, what the fuck they wanted with me and my family. I was actually met with a reply. The woman on the left spoke very matter of factly when she said, "We want you and your wife first. We'll come for that pretty little lady last."

I hadn't expected a response. I was stunned. I sputtered out a pathetic, "Why?"

"You've lived here long enough. And now it's time for you to really come home."

*Come home?* I had no idea what she was talking about. Just as I was about to reply, each of their heads turned to their left, and they looked past me at something in our room. I looked behind me, and saw a pair of glowing eyes in the bedroom. My wife screamed and I ran to shut the door on the smiling intruder, as it began to take a step towards us. Just then, the power came back on, and just like that, the smilers on the balcony were gone. The microwave started beeping.

I kept the bedroom door closed.

I told my wife we needed to get out of the area. It seemed as though the smilers would only show up during the blackouts. I didn't know if they could control the blackouts themselves, but it didn't seem so, otherwise why wouldn't they just finish what they came to do in one attempt? We agreed that we weren't safe at the hotel anymore and packed our things. On our way out, the clerk who had checked us in asked what was going on? I don't remember exactly what I said, but it was something about the blackout. His response to me was, "What blackout?" I didn't stop to explain.

Before getting the hell out of Dodge, I thought it would be a good idea to go past our house to see if anything had happened there in our absence. As we drove by, we saw the front door and every window on the first floor wide open. All the lights were off inside but I could just barely see the glow of the display on the electronic components in the living room from the road, so it wasn't due to a blackout. I had left a few lights on before I left. I know I had. Instead of stopping to investigate, we just kept on driving, heading for the freeway.

We've been on the road for many hours now, heading east. We haven't seen anything yet, but it's also not night time.

3

\* \* \*

I suppose I was a bit cryptic last night when I said we'd been on the road. It took us three hours to make it to my in-laws' cabin. Although a cabin deep in the woods may sound foolish, I thought it to be a good place to go because there are four generators there. We stopped again at a Wal-Mart and stocked up on food, flashlights, water, other random supplies, and I bought two large hunting knives. Knives don't run out of bullets. We didn't pass anywhere that sold ammunition otherwise I would've stopped and gotten as much as I could carry. And, no, Wal-Marts where I live do not sell ammo.

We got to the cabin around 9-ish, so we were preparing for something to happen. We put our daughter to sleep in the family room of the cabin and stayed in there with her. I brought two of the generators into the room with us so they would be handy in the event of a smiler-caused blackout. We had all the blinds closed except one, so I could see one of the things flailing about towards us before it saw us.

The woods were pitch black beyond the solitary beam of light that shone through the uncovered window. The silence around us proved to be too unnerving to handle so I put a DVD I had bought in the player to have some background noise while my wife and I anxiously awaited whatever may or may not be coming for us.

It was around 12:30 that I jolted awake. I must have

dozed off while sitting there with Kimmy, who was now asleep. The power was still on, but the lights flickered. I quietly stood up and looked out the window. I saw nothing at first, then, in the distance, I saw two very small orbs of light appear. They were stationary for a moment, then began to bounce up and down. Then about a foot away from those, two more appeared, and two more, and two more. There must have been 40 of these lights, all starting as still as can be, and then proceeding to lightly bounce up and down.

I realized they were getting bigger as they bounced. And then again I noticed they weren't just getting bigger, they were getting closer. They were the smilers' eyes.

I couldn't see their bodies in the darkness of the night but their eyes shined like sparklers on the Fourth of July as they got closer. I saw the first ones' silhouette; it was big, bigger than any I'd seen before. And shortly after that, the rest came into my view. I woke my wife and told her to protect our daughter. It was then that the lights went out. I immediately revved up the generator and plugged the lights into it.

I looked out the window and the smilers had stopped advancing. They then let out an ear-shattering howl of laughter, as if someone had just told them the funniest joke they'd ever heard. In the middle of this, the generator shut off. I scrambled to start the other one, but all it did was rev; it never turned over.

I felt like this was it. I felt like they had us trapped. I took my phone out to hopefully leave something to let anyone know what happened to us.

I began taking picture with the flash on my phone. I pretty much just mashed the screen over and over, taking as many as possible. The scariest thing was, with each flash, I could see them perfectly, and every time a took a picture, they were in a different pose, each one different from the next. It was absolutely horrifying. They then let out another screeching laugh, this one startling me so bad I dropped the phone on the couch I was taking the pictures from. I picked it up, and when I directed my eyes back towards the window, a female smiler was standing there, excitedly waving at me.

It was then that we heard all the glass around us shatter. All at the exact same moment. I spun around and, due to the darkness, I could barely make out figures crawling through the drawn curtains. Their bodies moved, for lack of a better word, lackadaisically. They kind of threw themselves over the partition through where the glass no longer was, then flailed their limbs over. Luckily, it took quite some time for them to get through. I looked back at the window I was initially in front of, and for the first time, I saw a different expression on a smilers face. She had a look of pure surprise, raised eyebrows with a hand over her mouth. It looked sarcastic.

I grabbed the gun, and fired it directly into the

surprised looking ones' face. When the figurative dust settled, there was no smiler there anymore. A wave of confidence rushed over me mixed with shock. I'd never killed anything in my life before. I snapped back to reality when I heard my wife softly say my name. I turned around and there was the woman smiler, directly in front of me, only she wasn't smiling. She looked furious. There was pain in her eyes. She struck me with an open backhand, which had way too much power for the size of woman she was. And it sent me tumbling back.

I grabbed the knife out off of the table I landed next to and unsheathed it. The woman let out a lone laugh while the rest of the smilers advanced from the other parts of the house. I got up, my entire being comprised of fear, and I decided to go for broke. I lunged at the woman and swung my arm in a stabbing motion. As soon as the knife would have connected, she vanished, along with the rest of the smilers, at the same moment the lights turned on, and, inexplicably, all the generators began running, including the ones outside. I stumbled forward, nearly falling on my face, dropping the knife to the floor.

I immediately got my footing and rushed to my family's side. Though stricken to their core with terror, they were unharmed. My wife insisted we immediately leave and get to somewhere more populated. We got in the car and began driving. I asked my wife to look in my phone at the pictures I took, as I told her I wanted to get pictures of them for proof.

As frustrating as this is going to sound, each and every picture I took last night, was black. Not pure black like the camera wasn't working, but black like I was shining it into nothing, and wasn't using the flash. There is no other way I can think to explain it. I knew that when the smilers laughed after I took the pictures, it was because they knew the pictures would be black. My daughter was in tears over the events. My wife moved to the backseat so they could comfort each other.

I don't know what to think about this night's events. After my daughter fell back to sleep, my wife and I began to talk and decided we should split up. That maybe it was one of us drawing the smilers. That maybe it was only me, since I was the only one who saw them the other night while driving to the hotel.

We bought a beater car decent enough to get my wife and daughter to her parents house today, while I will be staying at a hotel nearby in case something does in fact happen to them. I have also contacted a paranormal researcher who will be meeting me at my hotel. He has agreed to stay with me for the night to hopefully witness what has been going on. In addition to this, because I stressed the urgency of everything going on, he said he would make my case priority one, and do some quick research into my family as well as my house before meeting with me.

As always, wish me luck. Thank you.

4

Last night, the paranormal researcher came to stay with me at the hotel I was at, and much to my surprise, he brought a priest with him. I chose to get a first floor room, since I knew that being on a different floor didn't hinder the smilers from getting to me. I kept in constant contact with my wife, who, as you'll soon find out, didn't stay at her parents house for the night.

The researcher, whose name is Paul, gave me an overview of what I was dealing with. Since it was still daylight, he felt as if we would be okay discussing the situation at the hotel since we were already there.

Paul explained to me that the house was a threshold. What were were dealing with was a sort of skin-walker-ghost hybrid. They inhabit recently buried bodies, which explains their overall dirty look. It was not clear how my family was involved. The priest, Father John, asked if anyone in either of our families had recently passed, and the answer was, "No." I had my wife on speakerphone while we spoke about this. The only conclusion we could come up with was that the smilers had us mistaken with another family. Kind of a cop out if you ask me, but at least it was something.

Paul and Father John urged me to accompany them to

my family's home. If we were going to understand what was happening, it would be best to go to the source.

We made the hour long trip back to the house. When we got there, the doors were shut and all the blinds were drawn. It was on the brink of dusk, so we hurried into the house and made sure the power was on before we ventured past the foyer. The first thing Father John and Paul did was walk around and unplug everything that could be used as a source of light. This pretty much included any and everything that was plugged in. Next, Paul salted all the entryways. I felt stupid for not doing this before at the cabin.

While Paul salted, Father John and myself lit roughly 150 candles throughout the house. Father John was nice enough to have brought those along with him. That's when my wife and daughter pulled up in the beater car.

There was a brief moment of tension, as I didn't want them in harm's way, but my wife gave me the sort of look that said, "I'm not leaving." And that was that.

My daughter sat on the couch watching a DVD on a portable DVD player. She knew it would have to be shut off when it got dark. Something that Paul suggested was that the smilers fed off of electricity. We got as prepared as we could, given the circumstances. Father John armed each of us with holy articles, and kept a small container of holy water on each platform that surrounded us in the living room.

163

The sun set. Night blanketed over our neighborhood, and I don't know if it was just me and my nerves, but it seemed darker than ever. My daughter had put away the portable DVD player, and we turned off all our phones except for Father John's, as we figured having one line of communication would probably be a good idea. We basically all huddled in the middle of the living room while my daughter slept on the couch, our house illuminated dimly by the throes of candles we had lit.

It was about 1 AM when everything started. Paul happened to be looking out the window when the street lights on either side about three houses down suddenly went out. He got my attention, and the rest of us rushed over. The next set of lights went out. It was between this set going out and the next one that we finally saw them. Limbering along in the Bernie-esque fashion they do, eyes glistening in the moonlight. I immediately saw the fear in Paul's eyes. He voiced his concern. "I know I said what they were, but I've never seen one before."

At least he could see them. I sent my wife over to protect our daughter. Through all of this, their safety was my only concern, whether it seems like it or not. As the smilers approached, I found myself once again frozen while my eyes locked onto a set of theirs. I was shaken by Father John and we went to the middle of the room and anxiously awaited the smilers to reach the house. Sadly, there wasn't much we could do.

While the smilers slowly flailed their way towards us, I confirmed that both Paul and Father John had seen them, then asked why the cop couldn't. Father John and Paul concluded that it must be the house itself that makes people besides myself and my family capable of seeing them. Another semi-answer. I asked Paul if he had gotten any information on the house, and he said he had only had time to do a quick Google search on the property, and was unable to delve further into its history and past occupants. I felt like that was where the answer lied.

The smilers eventually made it to the yard, and that's when they stopped walking and began waving, smiling all the while. All but one. It was the female that had let out the laughter the night before. She just stood there, back arched backwards, arms hanging behind her. She was expressionless. She hobbled her way up to the front door, and knocked. Plain as day, as if she was a UPS driver, just knocked on the door. None of us moved. Then she pounded on the door. And kept pounding. And didn't stop until my wife screamed "What?!" We were met with silence, until the woman smiler broke it.

"It's time for you to go."

Father John responded. "This is not your home! This family owes you nothing! Be gone!"

The smiler let out the same shrill laughter I'd heard the night before. It was horrifying, and a sound I will never be able to forget. The other smilers crept up to the windows, all but one of which was covered by curtains. They started banging on the windows, but not breaking them. Now that I think about it, even their walk was less exaggerated than it normally was. They weakly banged on the windows, while their female leader gave us a warning.

"You can not keep him out of where he belongs forever."

Father John asked, "Who?" And then it was over. The smilers were gone, and the street lights came back on. We all breathed a deep sigh of relief. But yet again, I was met with more questions than answers. Why was it time for us to go? Who was I keeping out of where he belonged?

Now, I love my wife dearly. She and my daughter are my everything. But even with the warnings I had stressed to her, she made a foolish, no, a stupid decision. For whatever reason, while we were all collecting ourselves, she walked over and opened the front door, presumably to check the porch and verify the female smiler was gone. Don't ask me why. I will never know what compelled her to do something so ridiculous.

As soon as she turned the knob, Father John yelled, "No!" But it was too late. The door flew open and pinned itself against the wall behind it at the same time the street lights went out again. There stood the female smiler, only she wasn't smiling. She looked rabid. She was breathing heavily, her eyes were popping out of her head, and her fists were clenched as she, for the first time I'd ever seen a

166

smiler do, leaned forward. She looked down at the archway of salt.

"Move the salt and we will show you mercy."

"Mercy for what?! What have they done?!" pleaded Father John as he held up a rosary. He moved closer, and his presence did seem to have an effect on the smiler, who returned to her normal position, back arched backwards, arms hanging.

"We have been nice enough, you have been the one to take issue." She said, as she flung her arm up and pointed her crusty finger at me. All I could think was, "No shit I took issue, dirty ghost zombie demon limp walker assholes have been trying to take my family to do God knows what with."

Father John retorted, "You will not haunt this family into submission!"

She stood there in silence for a moment, before opening her large mouth to reply. But as she began to speak her first words, every candle in the house blew out, and she disappeared. Right before our eyes, like someone had flipped a switch. The street lights once again came back on, and the light poured in through the door and the one uncovered window. None of us could move. We all stayed where we were for what felt like an eternity. The sound of my daughter crying broke the silence and my wife went over to comfort her. The three of us men reconvened in the middle of the living room, and it was obvious. We needed to know about this house in order to figure out what to do about the problem.

As soon as the sun is up, Paul and Father John are going to go out and do their research. My family and I are going to stay in our home, guarded by the salt which seemed to do the trick. We are going to make sure to keep all electricity use to a minimum, as we don't know if the smilers potentially charge during the day then reveal themselves at night.

I will relay the information I get to you tomorrow, as well as any events that may or may not occur tonight. This has been a terrible few days, but for the first time throughout all of this, I feel like we may be on the path to the end.

Once again, thank you all for your help and well wishes, and as always, wish us luck.

5

My family and I spent the day at home, and it was ultimately an extremely boring day. Father John and Paul were out doing their research while we essentially sat in silence all day. We had been advised to use electronics sparingly, so that took out any kind of entertainment we had, save for board games. To be honest, we've become too accustomed to technology to have that entertain us for any real length of time.

Father John and Paul got back to our house at around 3 in the afternoon, and they came with information. Our house was built in 1955, and no, the land was not once a cemetery or ancient Indian burial ground or anything. The problem lies in a past resident. When we bought the house, we knew it hadn't been lived in for quite some time. Nearly a decade. Apparently, houses in the neighborhood stayed vacant for quite some time before someone who decided they could live with the blackouts came across them. The last occupant of the house was a man named Lee Ruechell and his family. Lee and his wife, Georgia, were elderly, and their daughter, Carrie Anne, stayed with them to take care of them in their old age.

With this information, Father John and Paul were able to dig into the occupants. Lee suffered from Hodgkin's Lymphoma and was an active member in the church community. Lee was a very well-liked man. When there was an issue with his social security, other members of the church banded together and took over his mortgage for him for nearly a year. It seemed as if he had a bit of a dark side, though. His wife and daughter were admitted to the hospital several times throughout their lives for what looked to be domestic abuse related injuries. On the outside, all seemed well, and his wife was a loyal one, and his daughter a caring one. Even though they had their problems, they were still a tightknit family. Lee died from his disease, in the house, in 1992. It wasn't revealed in which room or anything, but at least that was something.

Georgia and Carrie Anne spent the next year together in the house, and apparently they got heavily involved in the practices of seances and speaking with the dead, in an attempt to locate Lee. This information was found due to a small fire that had happened in the kitchen, which was the result of candles being used during one of the seances. The realtor had informed us of the fire when we were purchasing the house, but didn't reveal to us the cause. We thought nothing of it; it had been fixed, so we didn't give it a second thought.

In late 1993, Georgia passed away from natural causes in the city hospital. The house was inhabited solely by Carrie Anne for the next 6 months, and continued to be the site of many communications with the dead. For unknown reasons, Carrie Anne moved away, and the house sat vacant until we bought it in late 2013. Carrie Anne committed suicide last week, and was buried in the cemetery in a plot next to her parents.

Father John and Paul then gave their opinions on what they felt the issue was. They are under the impression that with the death of Carrie Anne, the Ruechell family is now back together, and they want their house back. We thought back to when I was spoken to for the first time. "You've been here long enough, it's time to come home." Father John and Paul came to the conclusion that those were two separate statements, as in, "You and your family have been here long enough. It's time for us to come home." I know this is a long shot, but it would fit the scenario if this was the case.

As far as them suddenly getting violent, it's thought that it was due to my apprehension to let them in. They had smiled and waved, in a gesture of friendliness, and I had taken it the wrong way. When we left the house, they knew we would eventually come back, so they showed up at the hotel, and then the cabin to continue to persuade us to leave the house for good. When I shot the smiler through the window, it angered them. So they broke all the windows and came in, and were prepared to attack. Our guess is that due to the limited energy being used at the cabin, they couldn't defend against the knife attack, so they disappeared when I attempted to stab the woman smiler.

As for what was said last night, the whole, "You can't keep him out of where he belongs, forever." That was probably the angry side of Lee Ruechell coming out, demanding he get his home back. Our guess is that the large number of smilers are spirits that Lee has befriended in the afterlife to help in the effort to get his home back.

Mind you, this is all conjecture. All evidence of what we're assuming this to be is circumstantial at best. For all we know, we could be totally off. I think that might be the scariest part. What we do know for sure is that the salt worked. It fended them off last night. Also, the smiler seemed to respond to Father John's rosary, so that was a good second line of defense. The problem is we can't control the power outside the house, so the smilers can still get their energy from the surrounding houses. Even if we did cut off all power to our house, that wouldn't keep the smilers out.

Despite all of our headway concerning the puzzles of the previous nights, we have no idea why the smilers approached my wife and daughter first. Our only thoughts on that, are that some of the smilers aren't necessarily on the same mission as the rest. Some of them may have ulterior, sinister motives. I have to say, it's extremely frustrating not knowing what exactly it is we're dealing with, and working only off of semi-educated hypotheses.

\*\*\*

We reinforced the salt barriers and relit all the candles throughout the house, in preparation for whatever the night brought. We then just waited, each taking turns sleeping while others kept an eye out.

Nothing happened until about 3:30 AM. Father John woke me up, and told me he had heard something upstairs. We looked out the window, and from what we could see, all the power was on outside in the street. Myself, Paul, and Father John made our way upstairs, each armed with a holy articles. We searched the upstairs but found nothing.

As we were heading back downstairs, the door to the

attic, the kind that swings down and drops a ladder, did just that, sending the ladder down with a loud crash. We nearly jumped out of our skin as we turned around. An angry looking smiler bobbed his way down the attic stairs. Father John started saying a prayer, while Paul and I held up our articles.

This smiler seemed partially phased by the religious moment. He didn't stop moving. Instead, he almost tiptoed towards us, backing us down the stairs. He kept his distance, though. I finally spit out, "What do you want?"

Just then, two more smilers came tumbling down the attic steps, like they had fallen. They got to their feet and moved ahead quickly behind their angry friend. Suddenly, the smiler behind the one that was slowly approaching us, pushed the one closest to us directly into us. It hit Father John's cross and let out a shriek, and before it disappeared into thin air, it knocked us backwards down the stairs, and we all fell, step after step.

The two remaining smilers threw themselves down the stairs, just like we had, only voluntarily. They landed nearly on top off us and got back up as if nothing had happened. They ignored us while we writhed in pain, too shaken up to realize what was happening. Once in the line of sight of my wife, she screamed. One smiler made a beeline for the front door, and the other went for a side window in the room opposite the living room. They both stopped before the salt, inhaled deeply, and blew the salt away, effectively opening the barriers between us and the rest of the smilers that I realized were now outside.

It was then that I noticed every light in the neighborhood was out. Every street light and every house was completely pitch black. I managed to stand, and that's when I saw. What seemed to be an entire night sky of stars worth of bouncing, glowing eyes was making its way towards our house from every direction. Father John quickly got up and ran to the smiler at the front door, pressing his rosary against it, causing it to dissipate.

I followed suit and lunged at the smiler by the window, doing the same thing, successfully. Father John put his back to the door, but was sent flying forward when the door was broken off of its hinges. The woman smiler I had come to know and hate so much stood there before me, smiling her muscle-stretched smile.

I don't know what I hated more, the smile or the angry face.

Paul asked what the smiler wanted. She simply replied "Uninterrupted access to our home."

"Are you Carrie Anne Ruechell?" Father John inquired.

"No, I am Georgia Ruechell." The smiler retorted.

"This is no longer your home, be gone!" Demanded the brave priest.

Georgia let out that shrieking laughter that could have shattered all the windows. Suddenly, Paul lunged forward from behind me in an attempt to hit Georgia with his rosary. She simply side stepped which resulted in Paul falling forward onto his face, into the outside. In an instant, he was swarmed by smilers, whose flailing limbs and falling bodies quickly blanketed Paul. All we could hear was his screams.

"We came in peace," said Georgia. "But you've left us no choice. The only way you get to reside here any longer, is as one of us. My husband is tired of your selfishness in this matter and demands you be dealt with in the most mortal of ways. If you had just given us our home back in the first place, you could've gone on about your life."

I didn't know what to say. I could only live here if I was dead and had my soul moved into somebody else's body?

"We will be back tomorrow evening, and it will be your last chance to accept your fate. Otherwise, you will be responsible for whatever pain my husband decides to impose on you and your family."

And with that, she was gone. The candles in our house blew out, and the lights in the neighborhood went back on. Had she basically told me that tomorrow night, we were going to die, one way other the other? Father John did say that he assumed the smilers had done this sort of thing before, but probably hadn't been met with such resistance. Paul was gone. He had vanished with the rest of the smilers. That is something that's going to weigh heavily on my conscience for some time.

Then, I had an idea. Since I'm essentially out of options, and am more than likely going to die tomorrow night, I decided to be proactive. Father John insisted against it, my wife hates the idea, and my daughter is terrified, but, I'm just thinking *fuck them*, I'll do what I have to in order to keep my family safe. I'm on my way back home with 5 gallons of gasoline. I will let you know what happens tomorrow.

Wish me luck.

6

This entire situation has been literally driving me crazy. I can't fight these things, I can hardly defend myself against them. I'd been essentially condemned by the de-facto matriarch of what I thought was mine and my family's home. I didn't know what else to do.

Father John blessed our house numerous times throughout the day, and prayed with my family and I as we mourned the loss of Paul, who gave his life trying to protect us. I will never, ever forget the sight of the swarm enveloping Paul. His pained screams will haunt me until the end of my days.

We disconnected the main power source to the house this morning. And then, we salted all the windows and doors again, this time not forgetting the window in the attic, or any in the basement. We had a plan for what we were going to do, and it required some finesse.

Father John got a collection of holy relics and set them up around the house in various places, and set jars of salt up on predetermined posts. We then armed ourselves with multiple toilet paper roll-sized tubes of salt which we holstered in our pockets. Kimmy remained practically silent throughout everything. I could tell this was taking a severe emotional toll on her. All I wanted was to do was protect her and Anna.

The gas tanks were sitting idly by in our kitchen, I still wasn't sure what the plan was with those. I mean, I had an idea, but like I said, it was going to take some grace to pull it off. We waited in the dark, lighting only a few solitary candles in the living room. Then we twiddled our thumbs.

The smilers wasted no time. The entire street went black—all street lights and houses. It seemed darker than usual. Even though the moon was out, it was as though the darkness was overtaking the light. One by one, sets of glowing eyes appeared down the street in either direction. As usual, we kept all the curtains closed except one set, which was for sighting purposes. We had to see when they were coming.

The glowing eyes grew brighter as the smilers flailed towards us, until their silhouettes appeared in a visage I wish I had never laid eyes on. There must have been fifty or sixty smilers in the street. Each one sported a foul grimace, one that said they were now beyond the apparent pleasantries they had initially approached us with. How they thought their initial appearance was in any way welcoming is beyond me.

From the left, I saw one smiler in particular leading the others. I took this to mean that this smiler in particular was the Lady Ruechell. Then, all of the sudden, behind the group that paraded around her, was, as far as I could tell from a distance, a male smiler, bigger than I'd ever seen, who, while still somewhat lazily flailing about as he moved, seemed to have a much smoother and more connected way of movement about him. While the smilers I had seen up to this point had such an exaggerated way of getting to where they needed to go, as if they were being controlled by a marionette, this bigger fellow moved about as though he were a stumbling drunk. I know those don't sound too different, but trust me, the distinction is apparent.

I immediately made the connection, and alerted Father John that I was relatively sure that Lee Ruechell himself was joining the show. We got ourselves armed with rosaries and approached the spot where my front door was propped up against the doorframe, having been broken off it's hinges the night before. It felt like an eternity as they made their way down the street. Once they were finally nearing our property, Georgia let out screeching, howling laughter. As they continued approaching, they spoke.

"I must say, I'm quite surprised to see you here!

Though, we would have found you anywhere!"

Before I could even process what was being said, Father John spoke up.

"We wish to come to an agreement!" He hollered at the top of his lungs.

Georgia retorted by mimicking her first laugh, and was joined by a new, much deeper laugh.

"My husband wants to meet the man who denied his extended hand," Georgia announced.

"I didn't mean to disrespect anyone! I didn't know what you wanted! All I was trying to do was protect my family! We will happily leave!" I yelled, hoping to come to some kind of understanding.

I was met with no reply. I stood there, breathing heavily, anxiously awaiting a response. After about 30 seconds of silence, I took a peek through a crack between the propped up door and the frame. I jumped back when I was met with a stare from both Georgia and Lee Ruechell. There was something about the smilers' eyes that always absolutely captivated me the moment I first looked into them. I broke my gaze and stepped back, moving the door away from the frame, confronting the enemy once and for all.

"We will leave. Please." I pleaded.

"I find your resilience inspiring. I can't simply end your existence. I would require you to become a member of my group. Move the salt."

"This family has done nothing to you." Father John explained. "They were simply frightened by your abrupt appearance and—"

He was cut off by a low pitched yet very loud growl by Lee Ruechell. I'm assuming this was because he didn't particularly care for a holy man to be speaking to him.

"I have made my decision. Now remove this salt. There is nowhere for you to go that I will not send my subordinates to find you."

There was a tense silence for what seemed like an eternity. I looked over at my cowering wife and daughter in the living room as tears filled my eyes. This was it.

"May I have a private moment with my wife and child?" I politely asked.

"Remove the salt and put down the crosses you've armed yourselves with. Then you may do as you wish."

I reluctantly slid my foot over the salt, brushing it away in every direction. Each of the four of us slid our rosaries across the floor, away from the Ruechells.

Lee, Georgia, and a third smiler that hadn't yet spoken and I hadn't yet seen hobbled in. I presumed this to be Carrie Anne.

"Home sweet home." said Lee, in a repulsively smug tone. "You will take your moment here, in front of us. Then we will commence the evening." The Ruechells took a look around at their new old house, while being sure to not get too far away from us.

"Father, pray with us." I all but demanded. The four of us huddled mere feet away from our soon to be killers, I didn't know what they were going to do to us, but I knew it wasn't going to end well. I only hoped it would be fast. I couldn't bear thinking of what my sweet daughter could be moments away from, or that we would soon be suffering the same ambiguous fate as Paul.

I whispered to everyone. "I just saw Brian go past the back door. As soon as he makes it to the front, we go."

Father John whispered a prayer as I kept my eyes focused on the side window of the house, waiting to see a shadow rush past. It seemed like it took forever, but it happened. I waited about another two seconds, before I whispered "Go."

We began what felt like a slow motion dash through the hallway and into the kitchen. Behind us, I heard a roar from Lee. None of us hesitated. We reached the kitchen, which contained the back door. I had left the caps loose on the gas containers, and as quick as I could, tipped all five over, flooding the kitchen and the hallway with the pungent substance.

Father John flung the back door open and we tumbled outside. The Ruechells were quickly behind us, but stopped at the doorline and stumbling back into the kitchen.

"What have you done?" Lee demanded to know.

I didn't even think to answer him before I lit a book

of matches on fire and tossed it into the kitchen, setting home ablaze. We ran around to the front yard, avoiding smilers that seemed to just be standing there, mesmerized by something we couldn't see. Father John of course saw nothing, as he was no longer in the house.

We reached the front yard to meet Brian, Paul's brother: a paranormal enthusiast, himself. He had tried to make contact with Paul and knew how to get in touch with Father John in the event that Paul would not answer. We explained to Brian what had happened and he decided to finish what his brother had started.

As the fire raged through the house, a small explosion lit up the sky. It was most likely the propane tank on the back of the house.

Brian's part in our plan was integral. While I talked to the Ruechells in the house and took a "moment" with my family and Father John, Brian ran around the house, pouring out two gallons worth of blessed saltwater Father John had provided him with earlier in the day. That's what trapped the Ruechells in the house. The front and back doors were covered—no escape once they entered their beloved home.

As I heard roars and ear shattering screams from within the house, the rest of the smilers just stood there. And before we could even blink, all but maybe three or four of them were gone. The remaining smilers then simply turned around and flailed in directions, all away from us. We are not sure who these lucky "survivors" were or why they didn't disappear with the rest, but my guess is that they were ones that were not directly connected to the Ruechells and their mission. Again, strictly conjecture, I don't know if I'll ever know for sure. Without waiting to see the rest of the house go down in flames, but not before the roars and screams from within subsided, we all got in our cars and drove away.

I am now in a town about 80 miles from our old house. We received a call alerting us that our house was on fire. I explained that we were currently on vacation, and that this was a surprise to us. I had only hoped that none of my neighbors saw us drive away, but I'm sure I'm not that lucky, I have an idea of what I'm going to tell the police regarding why there was an obvious gasoline-fueled fire that occurred at my home, which I am choosing not to post here.

I have a sneaking suspicion that we're going to be quite busy in the times to come.

Both myself, my wife and daughter, Father John, and I'm sure Paul, would like to thank those of you that took time out of your lives to read about our plight. This hasn't been my most rational week, I assure you. I was doing what I felt was best for my family and I, and if, God forbid, you ever find yourself in a situation of similar magnitude, perhaps then you will understand some of the seemingly nonsensical things I did, and why I did them.

This all could have gone a lot worse, I'm sure.

To all of you, continue to help those in need. You will never be forgotten.

From the bottom of my heart: thank you.

And for good measure, wish me luck!

# Playing the Game of Seven Doors

## By Katie Irvin Leute

---

1

I'm not sure how we started, or who had the idea first, but when I was in middle school I had a group of friends who would all go into the woods together past the race track and play a game we called "Seven Doors." This game involved one girl laying her head on the lap of another; the second girl would cup her hands over the eyes of the first girl to block as much light as possible from shining through their eyelids. We would all circle around them, seated on the forest floor, and chant softly, "Seven doors, seven doors, seven doors…"

The girl whose hands were cupped over the first girls eyes would ask her questions after we chanted for a few minutes. What do you see? Where are you? Do you smell or hear anything? All leading sensory questions that would paint a picture of a location in the mind's eye. The girl lying on the ground would begin telling us what she saw, describing what she was doing, even where she was walking. Usually every "session" like this started in a forest similar to the one we played in, except that the girl who was "traveling" would be alone.

Within the woods were seven doors, each one a different color; there was red, blue, green, yellow, orange, purple, and white. They were scattered, and usually the goal of each session was to find a door, open it, catalogue what was inside of it and get back "safely" to the "entry point," or the clearing in the woods that all of us originally arrived in when it was our turn to travel.

We only had 45 minute for lunch at school, so we would usually only have time for one person to go under per day. Originally, it was just for fun; we would giggle and chant and listen with rapt excitement and attention at the visual story the girl who was traveling that day would spin for us, finding all manner of animals and plants in the "forest." We respected the hunt for the doors; no one was eager to slip a discovery into their story until it felt right or made sense. Thus it took us two weeks to find three of the doors and explore a little bit of what was beyond each.

The Blue Door was found first, and it led to a deep valley lake, with short white houses cut into the cliff sides around the lakeshore. We hadn't delved deep enough yet to know if the small cliffside villages were occupied or not.

The Red Door led to a huge city, built from gold, terra-cotta type material, with towering buildings that connected and reconnected through complex bridges. Again, we had yet to encounter any sort of dwellers or people there. A few strange birds that followed our progress through the city any time one of us ventured into the Red Door.

The Green Door led underground, into a dank, glowing grotto, filled with soft phosphorescent fungus that wove across the ceiling like a webwork of fine jeweled thread. There was a single fire pit with a crackling fire lit at the water's edge, and a small tent suitable for one or two people at the most furthest place within in the darkness.

We were slowly moving beyond the point where it was a game. In the beginning, perhaps we had tapped into the effectiveness of soft repetitive noise and some sensory deprivation by blocking the light from the eyes, and achieved some very mild meditative states. It may have helped with our intuition, our ability to get lost in our world that we all created together. Like a creativity exercise done to stimulate those more abstract portions of the brain that we are so plugged into as younger kids, and lose access to as we get older. Maybe we were just at that right age; not quite children anymore, not quite grown, but in-between. A gray state of being; transitional creatures each with a foot in two different worlds.

Maybe this is what made us susceptible. Who knows?

I remember going under on a Wednesday, when my turn came around. My friend, Jay, had her fingers cupped loosely against my cheeks. She had been taking guitar lessons, and I remember how calloused her finger pads were against my twelve year old skin. It made it harder for me to concentrate for a while, to sink into that soft fuzzy half-awake state that made it easier to immerse myself. A flash of irritation shot through me but I quenched it, squeezed my eyes shut, and tried to concentrate. The anticipation in the circle around us had changed in the last week. No giggles or smiles; we used to make faces at each other across the circle to try and get one another to crack the chanting with a laugh, but the last few days everyone had intently stared at whomever was on the forest floor, focused. Resolved. There was a mystery there and we were going to figure it all out.

Hindsight is 20/20. Isn't that what they say? If I could stop my twelve year old self somehow, I would.

Finally, the chanting stopped, and Jay asked me, "What do you see?"

The clearing was around me, as it always had been. I looked down and could see myself, wearing the flared Dickies and blue-striped, cap-sleeved shirt I had put on that morning. I circled around the clearing, getting my bearings. Our friend, Shina, had found the Green Door the day before, and she had turned twice before heading off into the forest. I was really curious about the grotto. I hoped I could find the Green Door again and spend a little more time exploring. I turned steadily, making a second complete circle, before walking out of the clearing into the woods.

It was midday; sun shafts broke through high canopies of thickly layered pine trees. Dead needles and rocks crunched under my shoes as I walked, threading in-between tree trunks and larger ferns. I described the landscape around me in colorful detail, until I was stopped short when Jay asked, "Do you hear anything?"

Huh. Besides my own footsteps, I hadn't thought about sounds. I paused, finally tuning in to the forest around me. There was a stillness, a heaviness to the forest that seemed to dampen all noise as if the sounds were trapped beneath a blanket. I waited, but besides me there was no sound. Not even one of the creatures my previous friends had identified in earlier explorations. My mind was a total blank.

"I don't hear anything," I whispered, and somehow saying it out loud filled me with a sudden blood chilling dread.

Ice in my veins, I slowly turned in a circle right where I was standing, peering sharply into the woods around me. This was… strange. Something was off. I didn't see anything out of the ordinary, but this weird, suffocating stillness seemed much different from the soft breezy forest we had come to know. I don't know why I was stupid enough to do this, but I called out, "Hello?"

A pause.

Then, in the distance, a sound. Leaves rustling?

The snap of a branch, so singularly loud in the stillness that it might as well have been a gunshot.

My heart cracked and fire surged through my limbs. I whipped around and began running back to the entry point, the clearing where we all entered and exited from.

*Fuck.* What was I thinking? I should have realized something was wrong right when I arrived but nothing had ever happened before, so why should it now?

My breathing came fast and hard as I dodged tree trunks and leapt over exposed roots. Jay later told me that I had called out "Hello?" and then started almost hyperventilating. She had been tempted to wake me up, but we had a rule about waiting until a person had returned back to the entry point before coming back. Something about exiting the same way we had entered, in order to keep everything structured and ensure that we had really "woken up."

I was mostly looking down at the path as I ran, to ensure that I didn't trip on a root or large rock. So when I looked up briefly, and saw a dark, hulking shape ahead of me in the woods, my heart nearly stopped right then and there.

"Shit!" I veered suddenly, dodging behind a pine tree, clutching the rough bark in my hands as I pressed myself against the trunk. I stuffed my hand in my mouth, stifling my gasping breaths, ears craning desperately for any sound. What was that? Were my eyes playing tricks on me? *What in the actual fuck was going on?*

I waited, hearing nothing but the thick silence and my own blood pounding in my ears. After a few moments, I cautiously peered around the edge of the trunk.

It was closer to me now. I hadn't heard anything, but there, in the direction of the dark hulking thing I had seen earlier, I could make out the distinct rectangular shape of a door.

"What is it? What do you see?" Jay's voice squeaked a little higher than normal.

"There's a door ahead of me," I whispered. I stared at it, fingers white-knuckled and stinging with sharp pain as the rough bark of the tree dug into them.

"A door?" A pause, then Jay spoke, her voice calmer, colored with curiosity. "What color is it? Is it green?"

I swallowed hard. "It's black."

It stood alone in the woods about 50 yards ahead of me. A dark, solid stain on which the light of the sun seemed not to touch. I couldn't see much else from my distance outside of a faint embossed pattern covering the center of the door.

There was a long pause. Then, another voice, from the

circle of our friends around us. "I thought there were only seven doors?"

"Elia, shhh!"

"Well she's changing the game! We haven't even found all the doors we decided to have yet and she's making more doors?"

I couldn't be sure, but somehow the door was getting closer to me through the woods.

"I'm running around it," I said, and began moving through the trees, circling around the door to the left. It didn't seem to move while I was looking at it, yet every now and then I realized that even though I was moving around and away from it, it somehow was closing the distance between us. When I realized that in the time it took for me to circle around it, it managed to halve the distance between us, I couldn't take it anymore. I broke my gaze, turned, and ran full sprint.

I was nearly at the clearing. *Just make it to the clearing and get out of here; it's a door, it's not like it's going to chase me—*

The trees broke up ahead of me, opening up into the clearing and my way out. I gasped in shaky relief, and slowed for a moment, peeking over my shoulder to see if the door was still following me. There was nothing behind me but trees and forest and I almost laughed.

"Guys! I think I lost—"

I turned, and screamed as I nearly ran right into it. It was three feet in front of me, and I barely avoided slamming right into it, throwing myself off to the side into the brush.

"Fuck, you guys," I cried. "Fuck, *fuck!* Jay, get me out, get me out!"

"Are you in the clearing?" Her voice was sharp.

I scrambled to my feet, and threw myself around the door, taking off into a hard run. The moment my toes passed the edge of the forest into the grass, I said, "Yes! Yes, get me out, now!"

"Five, four, three, two, one, and...open your eyes!" Sunlight nearly blinded me as Jay's hands lifted from my face and I scrambled up, frantically brushing dead needles off that had collected on my backside. I was panting. Jay's face looked pinched as she watched me. No one else said anything for a long time before Elia finally spoke up. "I can't believe you didn't open it."

"Are you shitting me? A creepy Black Door?" Remembering the sight of it chilled me and I shivered unconsciously. "No."

The bell rang, signaling five minutes until the end of our lunch time. "We'll try again tomorrow," Jay said quietly, and without another word, we got up and trudged back towards the school, a strange sobriety having fallen over everyone.

I almost didn't go to school the next day. Looking back, I should have stayed home and faked being sick.

2

When we met out in the woods the next day for our lunch time adventure, everyone was a little quieter than usual, but most of the girls had regained their good humor. I, however, had not. I had slept poorly the night before, waking multiple times throughout the night, drenched in sweat despite the Pacific Northwest dreary, forever-fifty-degrees weather. I had no recollection of my dreams, but it was hard to peel myself out of bed this morning. Needless to say, I almost didn't go to school, because I knew they were going to try again, and maybe even actively look for the Black Door. We were a curious bunch, and no one had seen it or experienced it besides me.

I was silent the entire way out into the forest, even when Elia shoved up next to me as we walked, digging an elbow playfully into my rib.

"Did the Black Door follow you home?" she mock-whispered.

"Elia, the day you take something seriously, is the day I die of shock." Aubrey had come up behind us and swatted at Elia's backside. Elia shrieked and leapt forward, skipping ahead of us while laughing.

"Should we call it eight doors now, since Kat found a new door?" This came from Emory, walking a little off to our left.

"No," I said quietly. "I don't even really know what

the hell I saw, but… let's keep it at seven." Somehow, acknowledging the Black Door's existence seemed like it would make things worse.

I wanted to pretend it never happened at all.

Emory fell into step beside me. "Did you see anything on it? You know, besides that it was black."

I shook my head. "Honestly, I wasn't looking super close. I think there were designs in the center, but of what, I don't know."

When we got to our spot in the woods, Jay and the other girls were already there. We formed our circle, with a girl named Lauranne taking the honored position of the traveller this time. Jay did most of the question-asking when it wasn't her turn to travel, so she knelt on the carpet of dead pine needles before Lauranne situated her head on Jay's lap.

"You ready?" Jay asked.

Lauranne nodded and shut her eyes. Jay cupped her hands and placed them over Lauranne's face. She took a deep breath, shut her own eyes for a moment, and then nodded briefly. The circle of girls began chanting.

*Seven doors, seven doors, seven doors…*

After a few minutes, Lauranne's breathing had become slow and heavy, as if she were sleeping; we could see her belly rising and falling beneath her baggy Soundgarden shirt. Her hands fell open and slack at her sides, her feet splayed gently outward. She looked deflated against the forest floor, as if she were a discarded doll with all the stuffing ripped out. Jay's voice cut through our chanting and all our voices fell silent. "What do you see?"

Lauranne let out a slow breath. Her voice sounded tiny as she said, "I'm in the woods. In the clearing." A pause, and then, "I don't see any doors. I'm going to start walking west."

"Do you hear anything?"

Pause. "There's a breeze; really slight. I can hear the leaves rustling. But nothing else."

"Do you see the Black Door?"

This came from Emory, and Jay looked sharply across the circle at where Emory was sitting. It was against the rules for anyone besides the question-asker to say anything or ask questions, to prevent any confusion when trying to "pull" someone back out of the imaginary woods. Lauranne's face furrowed slightly beneath Jay's hands, and Jay quickly repeated Emory's question to get everything back on track. "Do you see the Black Door?"

Lauranne seemed to wait for a moment before answering, and my heart began to pound.

"No. I don't see anything like a Black Door anywhere around me."

Lauranne continued to wander the woods for a while. She spotted a previously identified creature, a white stag, in the distance. It looked like a normal four pointed stag when we first saw it weeks ago, only it had a third horn spiraling straight from the center of it's head, in-between the two arching antlers. It always ran away if we walked directly toward it. It occasionally shadowed us, following off to the side as we made our way through the woods. Lauranne didn't even bother walking towards the stag when she saw it, and changed direction to continue walking. She noted that it began following her off to the side as it had done to many of us in previous journeys.

After a few minutes of this, Lauranne came to the edge of a previously undiscovered ravine. A small, narrow trickle of water cut through the forest floor below her, and after a moment, she announced that she was climbing down to the water.

"Is the stag still there?"

A pause as Lauranne "looked" around. "No," she said. "I don't see him anymore."

The ravine was dark and narrow, shallow enough to jump down, although once Lauranne was next to the river she noted that it was much darker than up on the forest floor. She began following the water south, describing roots and trailing moss sticking out of the sides of the ravine as she walked, overhanging branches and fallen tree trunks crossing over either side above her. After a few minutes, she said, in a little whisper, "I've stopped walking. I think it's getting darker."

It was silent for a moment. Even the woods around those of us in the circle seemed to have become still, the cries and noises of the lunch time chaos back on the school's grounds seeming to get further and further away.

"You mean the sun is blocked out from where you're standing?" asked Jay.

"No," replied Lauranne. "Like… like the sun is going down or something. Like it's getting later in the afternoon."

This hadn't happened before. Every time we journeyed, the sun was always at midday, bright and cheerful. Our gazes met nervously around the circle. "Do you want to continue, or head back?" asked Jay.

A long pause. We all held her breath. Then, "I'll continue for a little bit," said Lauranne. "But I'm going to start heading back towards the clearing."

Lauranne described walking a little further down the ravine, looking for a good place to climb back up. She said she found some knobby roots hanging out of the mud wall that looked like it would work well for handholds, when suddenly her breath caught.

"What is it?" asked Jay sharply.

"I think I see a door."

Alarm pierced through me, but moments later, Lauranne said, "It looks like yellow wood. Like a bunch of bleached, yellowing tree roots knotted together and woven into a door in the side of the ravine wall, across the river from me." Before Jay could respond, Lauranne added, "I'm going to try to swim across the river and get to it."

"I thought she was coming back?" I whispered to Emory next to me. Jay gave me a warning glare. We were supposed to be silent, but I wondered if Lauranne had heard Elia's "sissy" comment, because she went from being carefully cautious to suddenly diving into strange waters alone in an astral forest, ready to open a new door we'd never found before.

Lauranne described herself walking into the river water. The current wasn't terribly strong, and she waded out to the center, carefully stepping on submerged boulders scattered along the base of the river. She got out to almost her chest, when suddenly her relaxed, deflated body stiffened in a spasm, and she let out a choking gasp.

"What is it?" Jay asked quickly.

"It's *in* the river!" Lauranne's voice was a squeak. "Holy shit, there's a Black Door in the river! It's right underneath me! I almost stepped on it. Oh my god!" Her fingers were clenching and unclenching against the forest floor. "Oh fuck, I'm coming back right now. Shit! It's right there, how the—"

"Come back, Lauranne," Jay said sharply. "Hurry! Just get to the clearing."

Lauranne described herself turning and splashing inelegantly back to the shore, launching herself out of the water and climbing the roots up the side of the ravine. Her breath began coming in short, sharp gasps, feet twitching and hands scrabbling slightly against the ground. She said that she had gotten to the top of the ravine, had crawled away from the river on hands and knees and had turned around once, only to see that the Black Door was now at the edge of the ravine where she had just climbed up, towering against the backdrop of trees and sky and completely shadowing her from the sun.

"No, no, no," she began muttering to herself. "I'm running. Fuck, it's right behind me guys. What the fuck?" She began panting again, her chest heaving against the ground. I felt a cold sweat against the back of my neck, watching her. A few of us had grabbed each others' hands. We sat there, waiting; white knuckled in our circle.

After a few moments, Jay asked, "Is it still behind you?"

A short gasp from Lauranne. "Yes," she said. "Every time I look back it's—" A few more gasping breaths. "It's maybe ten feet from me." We waited, as she panted against the forest floor, her body wriggling and writhing in distress. Then, she let out a sharp cry.

"Lauranne?" Jay's voice was alarmed. "What is it?"

"It's starting to appear next to me. Off to the side. Just not there one minute and there again the next. Oh fuck you guys." Then she suddenly inhaled deeply. "I see the clearing!"

"Hurry," Jay muttered. "Just let me know once you're there."

Lauranne described looking over her shoulder and off

into the woods on either side a few times. As she neared the clearing, she said she lost sight of the Black Door. She checked the woods one more time as her feet crossed the threshold, before saying, "Jay, I'm here, get me  " her voice cut off with a horridly loud scream, loud enough that every girl in the circle jumped.

"It's in the middle of the clearing! Jay. Jay, it's opening."

"Five, four, three, two, one. Open your eyes!" Jay ripped her hands back off of Lauranne's face. Lauranne's eyes snapped open and she sat bolt upright, one hand clutching at her throat.

"Oh, Jesus," she said, gasping. "Oh, holy shit."

We all closed in around her, asking a million questions. *What did the door look like? Why was it following her? How was it opening, quickly or slowly? Did she get a glimpse of anything behind it?*

Once Lauranne caught her breath and calmed down a little, she said that it had begun slowly swinging outward as she stepped into the clearing, so she didn't get a good look at what might have been behind the door. She noticed a pattern on the door, especially the few times that it had gotten close to her, and with a shaky hand, she took a stick and drew a long, horizontal line, with three shorter lines beneath it, two that were right next to each other and the third one centered and a little below it. Around the lines she drew a circle. "That's all I can remember," she said.

"There was more but these were the biggest designs." She drew a shaky breath. "I know we're here to explore and learn, but you guys. I just. I didn't want to get near that thing." She shivered visibly. "There's something wrong with it."

The bell rang across the forest, and we all stood up, brushed dead needles from our clothes and began the slow walk back to the school. Lauranne was unusually pale, and she kept rubbing at her eyes. "Are you okay?" I asked.

"Honestly? Not really." She pinched the bridge of her nose as we walked. "I have a splitting headache. I kind of thought you were making up that whole 'Black Door' yesterday. You know, to make your session interesting." Her tone was slightly apologetic.

"I'm going tomorrow." Elia's voice cut across the air as she fell into step next to us. "I don't know why you didn't just open it and see what was inside."

"Yeah, you don't know, Elia," Lauranne retorted sharply. "The door felt. I don't know. It felt menacing. Like it was threatening me."

"I felt the same," I offered. "Like it was stalking me or something. It seems like it was a lot more aggressive with you."

Lauranne didn't answer, but the pinched look on her face spoke volumes.

"All the doors move," Elia quipped. "No door is ever in the same exact place twice. Maybe this one just moves a lot more than the others. We won't know anything about it until we open it, and not knowing just makes us more afraid." She squared her shoulders as we trudged back into the main building. "I'm looking for it tomorrow, and if I see it, I'm opening it up. I want to know for sure what's behind this Black Door."

3

I slept badly again that night. I kept hearing a faint knocking sound in my sleep, but whenever I woke up it would cease, and I could only hear the soft sounds of my parents and brothers sleeping in the rooms around me. At 3am I even got up, walked down to the landing and checked the front door, but no one was there.

My mom woke me up at 6:45am. My alarm had been blaring for the past five minutes, and I hadn't even heard it. She said she had to shake me a few times to get me up. I felt like my head was stuffed with sandpaper; at the time I didn't know what a hangover felt like, but looking back, I definitely peeled out of bed as if I'd participated in an all night rager.

It was dumping rain that day. When we met at lunch at one of the corner cafeteria tables, everyone immediately started talking about how we'd squeeze our next session in. The woods were completely out; it was raining hard enough that the ground would be muddy swampland for the next few days. It was Friday, and if Elia didn't take her turn that day it would mean waiting until Monday to find out what was behind the Black Door, if the weather cooperated. Frankly, I was kind of in favor of stopping the game altogether, but when I said as much, I got quite a bit of backlash.

"Kat, we know it's scary but we don't know anything about it. Maybe Elia's right and we're just scared of it because it's… you know, unknown." Emory softened her words with a peace offering of jo-jos from her plate, which I reluctantly accepted.

"I don't know, you guys. It's not just that we don't know what's behind it. We don't know what's behind at least four of the doors and even the doors we've opened are still a little bit of a mystery. It just feels so invasive. Like it's doing everything it can to get us to open it, almost leaving us no choice but to open it. It's not a door that we previously knew was going to be in the forest. And it showed up inside our clearing! I thought the clearing was supposed to be like a safe zone, where we pop in and out?" I stuffed a piping hot jo-jo in my mouth. When the world crashes onto your head, let the starchy warmth of spiced middle school cafeteria fries be your comfort.

"I brought that up to Jay last night on the phone," Lauranne said quietly. "She said technically we never decided to set the clearing as a safe zone, or whatever. Some of us just assumed it would be safe because nothing's ever followed us into it before."

Elia sat down next to me, slapping her lunch tray on the linoleum cafeteria table. "I just called my mom from the pay phone in the hall," she announced. "If you guys want, she's cool with having everyone over for a sleepover tonight." Elia rubbed her hands together, silent-picture-villainesque. "She's working a night shift so we won't even have to keep the screaming down." She winked at Lauranne, who coolly flipped her off.

A few had to check with their parents, including me. Shina said that she had plans already and couldn't make it.

Jay joined us halfway through lunch, apparently caught in a long lecture by one her teachers, and said she would definitely be at Elia's house later.

"Are you sure you want to do this in your house?" Aubrey asked. "I mean, we've always done it in the woods." She seemed about to say something else, but changed her mind at the last minute, and began stabbing at the steamed vegetables on her plate listlessly.

Elia shrugged. "Not my first choice, but I don't want to wait three days to find out what's behind the door. I'm worried if we wait too long it won't be there when we get back." She smiled wickedly. "Besides, if something follows me back to my house, maybe it'll eat my sister first."

\*\*\*

\* \* \*

Elia lived with her mom and older sister on the lower-south-side of my home town; not the wealthiest of neighborhoods, but still clean, respectable, and only a little run down. Her mom was a nurse who had been pulling late night/early morning shifts for the past two years, so she was on her way out once we were all situated, sleeping bags strewn over the tiny living room, with three ordered pizzas and a massive box of diet cokes on the counter. After repeatedly telling us to call her if we needed her for anything, she left. The moment her little Toyota pulled out of the gravel drive and disappeared down the road, everyone turned in silent unison and looked at Jay.

Jay scowled. "Can I finish my pizza first, you assholes?"

I was nervous, but strangely less afraid than I had been for the past few days. Somehow in the slumber party setting it actually felt more like a game again; my friends were all laughing and shoving each other as we all moved the furniture around to accommodate a circle of seven girls in the middle of the room, with Jay and Elia getting situated in the middle.

"Shina's going to be pissed that she missed this," someone said.

"Okay, everyone chill for five seconds. Should we light some candles?"

"Very 'light-as-a-feather, stiff-as-a-board,' Jay." I got up and helped Emory pull a few emergency tapers from the kitchen, setting them up around the outside of our circle seating area. Then we shut off the lights, and a rapt stillness fell over everyone as Elia settled her head in Jay's lap and shut her eyes.

We began chanting. *Seven doors, seven doors, seven doors…*

Elia sank quickly, her entire body melting like pudding against the carpeted living room floor. It was warm, still, the light soft and hazy, and in the past few weeks we had all gotten extremely good at chanting together, at the same tone and volume, creating a rippling wave of soft noise that fell into the background and grabbed your focus all at once. Elia was "out" almost immediately, but Jay waited for a bit before signaling us to silence and asking, softly, "What do you see?"

It was strange to hear Elia's normally brash, mischievous voice so tiny, so child-like and far away. "I'm in the clearing. Jay, it's really weird. The grass." She paused for what seemed like forever.

"What about the grass, Elia?"

"The grass is brown. Dead, dry, straw brown, like what happens to our lawn at the end of summer." Elia described herself touching the ground around her feet, and then walking to the edge of the clearing. She said that some of the leaves on the bushes right at the edge of the forest looked black, as if they had been burned.

"I'm going to walk south," she said. Elia made her way slowly, describing in elaborate detail everything she saw that might be noteworthy. Her intense personality was offset by a deep obsession with detail and a keen perceptive eye, and I had to admit that her journeys were some of my favorites, as she painted such a vivid picture for the rest of us.

The first ten minutes of Elia's journey were relatively uneventful. Here and there, she would see tiny patches of black underbrush, similar to the state of some of the plants at the edge of our clearing. Other parts of the woods were just as lush as ever, and she said she could hear birds, though she couldn't see any. She caught sight of what we had decided to call the green monkey a few weeks prior: a little primate-like creature with a long tail and peacock green fur that shone iridescent in the light of the sun, like the wing of a raven or crow. She called to it a few times, but it seemed content to peer down at her, head cocked from one side to the other as she whistled and coaxed. Eventually Elia grew tired of this little game and kept walking. The monkey didn't follow.

She claimed that the woods were beginning to get darker the longer she walked through them, similar to Lauranne's experience of time passing as she explored the forest in our previous session. We were so rapt in her descriptions that when she abruptly said, "I think I see a building," there were more than a few soft gasps from the circle. We'd found buildings through some of the doors, but we'd never found any sort of nonorganic structure in our woods before. Elia described what looked to be a large farmhouse or barn, settled in a part of the woods that was less densely populated by foliage than the rest. There seemed to be smaller trees arranged in neat rows to the east of the building, planted in a bare open plot of earth edged by the pine trees we were used to seeing in the forest. The dark wooden structure loomed three stories high, with windows looking out at each level, and a high pointed roof with rotting shingles covered in trailing green moss. There was one door at ground level.

It was entirely black.

"By black, you mean…" Jay looked uncertain.

"It's totally, solid black. It looks like there's writing or carvings on the front of it." Elia's voice quickened with excitement, and nerves. "It may be the same door Lauranne and Kat saw."

Everyone was silent for a moment. I could tell that Jay was searching for something to ask, when Elia said, "I'm walking toward it."

Aubrey grabbed my left hand and squeezed it.

"I'm walking slowly. I'm about thirty feet away. Now twenty." She paused. "The forest is really quiet again. I don't hear the birds anymore." A longer pause, followed by, "Okay, I'm going to keep walking. I'm about ten feet away. Now, I'm almost up to it—" Elia's voice cut off in a small little choking noise.

"What?" demanded Jay. "What? What is it?"

Elia let out a slow, unsteady breath. I'd known her for years, and despite all her bluster and bravado, I could tell that she was shaken by whatever she was looking at. "There's a bunch of symbols and carvings on the door. I see the pattern that Lauranne described. Lots of smaller shapes, lines intersecting making stars and weird holes, sort of like those illusion tunnels we drew with a protractor in art class. And...jesus... okay. So." Elia took a deeper breath. "So, there's also... a bunch of names."

"What names?" Jay was staring so intently down at Elia's face I don't think she even remembered the rest of us were there.

"It's. It's our names." A pause. "Our names are all over the door."

I'll never be able to fully describe the sudden, gut-puckering, hot and cold dread that sank from my head to my feet in that moment. It felt like someone poured live ants down the inside of my back. Aubrey was nearly breaking my hand with her grip, and I let her. My painful, squished knuckles were the only part of my body that wasn't crawling.

Elia described the location of each name; her's was right above the circle. My name was to the left of it, Lauranne's to the right, Jay's below. The other girls' names flared at different points in-between, creating a star of letters around a central symbol.

"I'll draw what symbols I can remember when I get

back," Elia said quietly. She took a shaky breath. "But I'm going to open it."

"Elia, don't!" Emory squeaked. Jay didn't even reprimand her. It was pointless. Her attention was solely on Elia's face, as were all of ours.

Elia described grabbing the black, round doorknob and turning it slowly. She said it felt warm against her palm, as if she were taking a person's hand. The door was silent as it opened, barely a whisper as Elia stepped back to pull it wide. Past the threshold, she could see what looked like the inside of a barn. Straw littered a dirt floor, and it was horribly dark, beams and support poles scattered around the wide open space in front of her.

"What else do you see?" Jay asked, breathless.

"Not much," Elia responded. After a few moments, she said, resolutely, "I'm going inside."

"Elia, stop it! Just come back, we saw what was inside and now it's over. You did what you said you'd do." I spoke without really meaning to, but again, Jay didn't reprimand me.

"I'm already inside. It smells like… well, a barn. Like horses and dirt and hay." Elia's voice grew a little stronger as the moment passed. "It's dark but there's still some light coming in through the windows. It looks like there's some stalls, and stairs leading up to a second floor. Everything is really…" She paused, as if considering her next words carefully. "Everything is gray. Even the forest outside the windows looks gray, like an old black and white movie." A pause, and Elia lifted her hand off the ground where she lay in her own living room. Then, "I'm looking at my arm and even my skin is white. Like, blanched white; there's no color anywhere."

She described herself walking towards the stairs at the back of the barn, looking around for a lantern or flashlight or something to help her see. After a few minutes, she stopped, and said uneasily, "I just noticed it now, but it's been happening since I walked in here. There's a weird sound going on in the background. I don't know how else to describe it. It's super quiet, but kind of low and choppy, with a kind of light rumbling beneath it." Her voice became distant for a moment. "Like I'm hearing a helicopter in an earthquake, but on the other side of the world."

Jay wasn't even asking leading questions anymore. We all just listened, silent, rapt, as Elia described reaching the stairs, and taking a hold of the railing. As her hand touched the bannister, she let out a sudden shriek.

"The door! Fuck, the door just slammed shut behind me. Jesus fuck, that scared me!"

"Elia, you need to come back, right now," Jay said forcefully.

"It's fine, it's fine… nothing else happened, I'm just. God, that fucking sound. It's still going. It's making my head hurt. It's like once I noticed it I can't stop hearing it."

Elia took a shaky breath, and then reached for the banister again. She climbed the stairs, eyes straining up through the darkness. It looked like the stairs wrapped around and led up to a third level, but as Elia climbed she casually glanced out the windows in the stairwell, looking out over the orchard.

Her breathing stopped for a moment. Jay gave her head a little shake. "Elia!"

She let out a huge breath and began breathing a little faster. "There's something coming through the orchard. Towards the barn. Like the shadow of a person, but not a person. Tall. Like almost as tall as the orchard trees." A pause, and then, "Okay, I'm getting the fuck out."

Elia turned and ran back down the way she came. She said she raced for the Black Door at the entrance to the barn, grabbed the knob, and flung it open only to see the same gray landscape stretching out ahead of her that she could see through the windows. The lush, colorful, green forest she had trekked through to get here was gone.

"Shit." Elia said she tried shutting and reopening the Black Door a few times, willing the green forest back into existence. Every time, it reopened to the colorless world, and when she glanced over her shoulder, she said the tall shadow was almost to the barn. "You guys! What the fuck do I do? Do I just walk through and try to come back the way I came? It's not the same forest." She gasped sharply, suddenly, and then almost squealed out "It's here. It's looking in the window at me!"

"Jay," I said in a panic. "Jay, we have to pull her out now!"

"The rules," she said, distressed. "I don't know what that's going to do! We're supposed to bring her back the right way or else something could go wrong."

"Do it, Jay," Elia said. "Oh god, please do it. Get me out. Fuck the rules. Just get me out now."

Jay sucked in a deep breath, and then, with a despairing look on her face, said, "Five, four, three, two, one, open your eyes!"

She pulled her hands back off of Elia's face as if they burned her. Elia's eyes snapped open, and she immediately sat up, hair disheveled and face pale.

We all stared at one another, a sick feeling of dread falling over us.

"Are you okay?" I finally asked.

"Yeah." She was quiet; she absently rubbed the side of her head. "Yeah, I'm fine. I'm… fine."

After we all calmed down a little, Elia drew what symbols she could remember from the door. To be honest, none of it made sense to us at all. Looking back now, some of it looked like sacred geometry that anyone might recognize, like mandalas and the tree of life.

Some of it was and still is gibberish to me. At that point, Jay suggested that we try to watch a movie to try and relax. Elia put in The Cable Guy and the mood lightened somewhat. Someone made popcorn but it mostly went uneaten. Three quarters of the way into the movie, almost everyone was in their sleeping bags and we all decided to go to bed at that point. But even though the lights were out and everyone was trying to lie still with their eyes shut, I could tell that hardly any of us was really sleeping. I kept lifting my head to peek over at Elia's sleeping bag, watching her breath rise and fall beneath the thick synthetic fabric. I couldn't shake the feeling that we had just really, seriously messed up somehow.

4

The weekend was a mess of anxiety and apprehension. I called Elia once on Saturday and on Sunday to check in on her and make sure she was okay; by the time I got her on the phone Sunday afternoon, she sounded pissed. "Look, it's sweet that you're all worried, but everyone's been calling me all day, all weekend. I'm fucking fine. I'll see you tomorrow." She hung up abruptly.

Jay was off hiking with her parents all day. I got a few of the others on the phone, but there were no solid theories on what we might have stumbled into. Elia wasn't talking much to any of us. It was 1996, so there wasn't much information on the internet, or even much of an internet at all; still, I got a call at 6 PM, Sunday night from Shina, who hadn't been at the sleepover on Friday but had been filled in on what happened.

"You got a sec?" she said when I took the phone from my mom.

"Yeah, we just finished eating. What's up?"

"Okay, so I've been keeping track of all the symbols that we've seen on the door. This afternoon I slipped into a chatroom on AOL called Esoterica. Usually it's just a lot of Wiccan fluff and throwback new age stuff from the 70's, but sometimes a few hard core occultists float through and spew nonsense for a while before being booted by a mod. I decided to scan in photos of that big symbol that Lauranne first saw in the middle of the door, and the other symbols that Elia remembered, and post them all to the room, just to see if anyone recognized anything or knew what it might be." I heard the shuffling of papers on the other end of the line. "Most of the conjecture didn't seem to go anywhere, but one guy, uh, user EnochLives77. He said some stuff that kind of made sense."

"EnochLives77?"

"Yeah." Shina sounded embarrassed. "This chat room was pretty intense. Like, people believing that they're vampires and stuff. That was definitely not the weirdest username I saw."

I sighed. "Okay, well what did Mister 77 have to say?"

"He said he recognized one of the symbols at the top of the door, the one that looked like spokes on a wheel; he said it was an old Sumerian sign called 'dingir.'"She pronounced it like "danger." "and that it meant, like… "God," or "deity." He said that if archeologists usually find it on plaques or carvings or whatever, and it comes before someone's name, then that means that person is some sort of deity or higher being."

"Sumerian?"

"Uh, like the oldest civilization. Remember in History class, we did that whole Mesopotamia thing, and we read Gilgamesh for two weeks?" Shina paused, adding, "Jay almost failed our final because she kept slipping her headphones in during the class readings? It was when she finally got Frogstomp, and she could barely function unless she listened to it at least twice a day."

"Oh, yeah. Jesus." I glanced over my shoulder to check and make sure my mom was still in the living room, and slipped into the hallway, dragging the phone chord with me. "How would anyone in a chat room know that?"

"They apparently geek out hard over this stuff."

"Okay, so one of the marks on the door means deity. Special super powered person. Did they say anything else?"

"Well, once we got on the Sumerian track, he mentioned that another symbol right below it could be one called…" More shuffling of papers in the background, and then Shina's voice butchering the pronunciation "… Usbalkit. He said that some people are still arguing about the meaning of some of these words. This one sometimes

217

means 'rebel' or 'revolt,' but it can also mean to, like, turn something upside down, or reverse it. He said he wasn't sure, but that the second meaning would make more sense in this case."

"So, what, the top of the door reads, 'God, reverse?'"

"No. No, it would be more like, 'God, upside down,' or 'the upside down god,' I guess."

Silence hung over the line. The quiet static of landline dead air hissed faintly in my ear drums as my heart pounded. Finally, I spoke up. "But this is just from some dude in a chat room, right?"

"Yeah." Shina sounded uncertain. "Honestly, Kat, none of us know what the fuck we're really doing here. I think it was fun when we started but now I just feel like, I don't know, like we're way out of our depth. Even if what this guy is saying is totally whacko, what you guys described that happened on Friday night. I just don't think we should play anymore."

"I don't either." I unwound the phone chord from around my finger; it has wound so tight that the tip of my index finger was starting to turn blue. "Okay, I have to go; I'll see you tomorrow. We'll talk about what you found out then with the others."

"Sweet dreams, Kit Kat."

"Ha! Bye Shina."

\*\*\*

* * *

I was late to school. My alarm once again failed to wake me and my mom was pissed; she told me she wouldn't let me stay over at anyone's house anymore if it kept throwing off my sleep schedule. I told her that I had been sleeping badly; she blamed the computer, and too much TV, and whatever else she could muster up, before telling me that I had to lay off the pop from now on. I kissed her cheek and slid out of the car without a word, heading towards my second period class.

By lunch time, I was dragging. My stomach was queasy, so I didn't even get food, but I bought a huge 16 oz Jolt cola before finding the table my friends usually sat at.

Elia wasn't there.

"She's at home sick," Aubrey reported, gravely. "Something about her stomach; her mom said she puked twice this morning."

We all stared at one another for a moment.

"Guys, this is getting really fucked up." I listlessly twisted and untwisted the cap on my plastic cola bottle.

"Yeah," Lauranne slipped a hand on my shoulder briefly. "I feel like we need to stop playing, but I also feel like we need to undo whatever the hell it is we just did, first." She absently rubbed her forehead. "I haven't been feeling well, either. Like, kind of sick. And I sleep like shit."

219

Surprisingly, everyone else started piping in; apparently no one in our group had gotten a solid night of shuteye in the past week.

"Well, if you'd like to sleep even worse, then pay close attention." Shina then related what she had told me the previous evening. She had pulled out her copies of the symbols Lauranne and Elia had drawn and spread them out over the table, pointing to the ones she was referring to.

After she was done, everyone was pensive. "We have to help Elia. There's no way she's just conveniently sick after going through the Black Door." Aubrey was staring down at the symbols, brow furrowed.

"So what do we do, exactly, to fix it?"

Everyone looked at Jay. She was chewing pensively on her lower lip, eyes thoughtful. "When we pulled her out, she was behind a door, and she couldn't see a way to get back to the clearing. Maybe we should try to send someone in and get back to the correct entry point. Maybe doing it the right way will set everything back to normal?"

Everyone thought about that for a moment. "And what if it doesn't?" Lauranne asked pointedly.

"Well, we don't have a better plan; we can't leave things the way they are. We broke the rules and I don't see how going back in could make it any worse at this point. But maybe we can make it better." Jay stabbed at the cafeteria spaghetti on her plate with her fork. "Anyone else have a better idea?"

Silence.

"Great. Then we're doing it."

Shina piped up. "So who's going to go in next?"

Everyone took that moment to study their lunch trays closely, avoiding eye contact with anyone else around the table.

"For fuck's sake," I said, exasperated. "I'll go in. We'll plan on tomorrow?"

Jay nodded. "Tomorrow, then."

\*\*\*

That night I fell asleep over my homework twice; each time, faintly, I swear I could hear a low, far off rumbling, just at the edge of my hearing, with a slightly louder *whop whop whop whop* layered over it. I'd wake up maybe 10 minutes after drifting off, my head splitting and my face crumpled forward against my textbook. The second time, when I awoke, I found I had drawn a small symbol in the corner of my spiral notebook paper: a single circle, with a long horizontal line across the top, and three smaller lines below.

The same symbol Lauranne had seen on the Black Door.

I felt that we were all spiraling; that Elia's current state would befall all of us if we just left things the way they were. I knew that if someone didn't do something, my own situation—and everyone else's—was only going to deteriorate.

Maybe there was no way out, really. But I decided that night as I settled in for a fitful round of sleep, that if this was my last time entering whatever realm we'd tapped into, then I'd try to make it count.

5

"Are you ready?"

My head rested against Jay's crossed ankles, eyes staring up at the sky beyond her head. It was a gorgeous day; crystal blue skies and wisps of white cotton clouds danced past the tops of the trees straight above me. It was actually warm for the first time in a long time; everyone around me in the circle seemed lit in soft fire as the afternoon sunlight broke through the pine trees and scattered like liquid gold to the forest floor beneath.

I took it all in for a second, and then sucked in a breath, shutting my eyes. "Ready."

*Seven doors, seven doors, seven doors…*

I was nervous. I had no idea how I was ever going to relax enough to slip into the altered state I had become so familiar with at this point, but suddenly it was happening; I sank, my vision receded into darkness, and the voices of the girls seemed to come from far away, as if I had dropped underwater. I shivered, and when I faintly heard Jay ask, "What do you see," I opened my eyes.

I was in a huge, expansive field. The sky, the tall grass that brushed against my jeans, the few small birds in the sky, all were gray, like I had stepped into an old black and white movie. All color leached from everything, including, as I looked down at myself, me. And when I raised my eyes, I nearly jumped; a sharp gasp escaped my lips, and from very, very far away, I could hear Jay's voice; "What is it?"

"I'm surrounded," I whispered. "They're all around me."

They stood on four legs, soft, sable fur glimmering in the dull grey light. Bristling antlers towered towards the sky, ending in wickedly sharp points, tipped dark with some unknown glimmering liquid. They looked like elk, but larger; and in the center of each velvety forehead, opened a third eye, unblinking and staring.

They surrounded me in a circle, and they were staring at me.

"Jay," I whispered. "Jay, what do I do?"

"Just move very slowly. And don't piss them off, please. We've got enough shit to worry about right now without adding to it."

I took a few hesitant steps towards one edge of the circle. The elk seemed disinclined to move, but as I approached, almost touching one of them, it shifted to the side slowly to allow me to pass. The circle closed behind me, and I could feel the weight of their enormous bodies, antlers clicking as they tapped against one another, moving in unison. Ahead, in the distance, I could see the tree line of a forest, and before that tree line, a huge building towered. Rows of smaller trees laid out across its front lawn like a small orchard. It reminded me of those plantation houses in the south, elaborate and impressive in its physicality, but also wilting, with crumbling shingles and dark moss claiming the corners of ceilings and the base of columns.

In the background, I started hearing a low, almost imperceptible noise; the low rumbling of a far off earthquake, and a softer chopping noise layered over the top.

I described it all to Jay as I began walking forward through the tall grass, the mansion looming up ahead of me. The low, rumbling sound encroached on the edge of my hearing; it was always there, subversive and barely loud enough to pick up, but for some reason the hairs had been standing up on my arms the moment I opened my eyes in the field. As I finished describing the scene for the others, I heard a faint sound coming from the building ahead of me. It sounded like a phrase. Like someone was repeating something over and over, but at the end of the jumble of words I could distinctly make out one syllable.

"Kat," it repeated with a jumble of words.

*Fuck.*

"Guys," I whispered. "I think I hear Elia's voice."

I took off in a light jog, booking it through high grass that slapped against my legs as I ran. Surprisingly, the herd of elk followed; they kept a medium distance behind me, but they moved like a silent tide over the field, spreading out behind me in a wall of antlers and muscle. As I approached the house, they fell back, marking a line about fifty feet from the front entrance with their bodies. They fell still, silently watching me as I approached the huge front porch.

The windows were dark; I couldn't see anything beyond the faded, cracked panes of glass. No sign or indication of what lay inside, waiting for me. The voice was a little stronger, yet I still struggled to make out the entire phrase. I simply heard a jumble of words, followed by "Kat," repeated over and over, in discordant singsong melody. Now that I was closer, I was even more certain that it sounded like Elia.

"There's nothing on the porch," I whispered. "It's bare; no furniture, nothing." As I approached the door, I balked: the front door loomed dark and heavy against the white wooden building, and I knew immediately that it was the at-once-familiar-and-dreaded Black Door. Yet something about it had changed. I swallowed, and stepped forward cautiously, the porch creaking softly under my weight.

The large symbol in the middle of the door was different from what Lauranne and Elia had described. There were still a circle, a long horizontal line and two lines beneath it, but where the third and lowest line had cut across the bottom of the circle, now it was replaced with a long outline of an ovoid shape, with a solid circle in the center of that shape. And as I looked, something dark stained the white wood wall next to the door. Maybe I was seeing things or recognizing a pattern where there wasn't any, but it looked like there was a hand print against the door frame; a dark central palm with long, ragged looking fingers stretching out, reaching in towards the door knob.

My eyes took it in, and that keening, rumbling noise at the edge of my hearing seemed to intensify, filling my ear drums. I found my right hand lifting, slowly reaching out towards that hand print. My limbs were shaking; my whole body shook. My organs and my heart and my lungs, rumbling and quivering and becoming that noise, until I heard nothing else and saw nothing else as I reached, palm desperately wanting to press into the blackness of its hand.

Pain exploded on the side of my body and I was launched sideways, sprawling over the porch, wrists and head slapping against the wood like a rag doll. One of the members of the elk herd had climbed the porch and stood towering over me, antlers shadowed against the gray sky behind him. It stared down at me as I gasped for breath on the ground, ice in my lungs, my head bursting with pain and my ribs bruised.

Jay's voice seemed to whisper from far away. "What happened?"

"I. Fuck, nothing. I just need to get out of here fast." The elk snorted at me, and I perceived a contemptuous note in its heavy breath, before it backed off the porch and stood in the grass in front of the mansion, watching me, impassively.

I scrambled to my feet, and approached the door, keeping my eyes off the grotesque hand print and reaching for the door knob. I noticed with trepidation the names of all my friends carved into the wood, and at the top of the circle, where Elia had claimed her name had been, I now saw the name "Katherine."

I opened the door.

The mansion expanded around me, massive. The ceiling was as high as a Cathedral, with arching points and angled apexes; nothing at all like what it might have looked from the outside. Everything was pale white, but there was an insidious darkness that hung heavy, coalescing in every nook and cranny and settling, as if it were waiting for me to do something.

Because of the unique architecture, there were corners everywhere, not just in the walls but on the ceiling as it sloped and dipped, arched and folded and met itself again in high peaks pointed up towards the sky and beyond. The massive space was decorated with strange furniture unidentifiable to me, and again, there seemed to be extra edges to things, as if I were looking at one of those Magic Eye pictures where illusions pop out of flat spaces. I developed a headache as my eyes tried to make sense of it all, and couldn't.

There were two staircases lining the walls, leading up to a second floor balcony and dark hallways beyond. Ahead of me at the far end of the large entryway seemed to be a huge, looming structure. A structure that I felt an immediate aversion to—a sick, gut-deep revulsion shook through me every time my eyes tried to focus on it. It seemed a tangled mess of angles and shapes that moved with slow undulating purpose out of the corner of my eye, yet when I grew close to looking at it, it went still, an indecipherable statue in an indecipherable room.

At its base, hunched over in a curled ball, was someone that looked like Elia.

"Jay! I see Elia. Jesus. She's still in here." I kept my eyes on her form, refusing to look at the large structure she was huddled in front of any longer. "I'm moving towards her; maybe if I get her out of here, this whole thing will be over."

A garbled whisper hissed in my ear. It sounded like Jay, but it was as if she were talking over a malfunctioning walkie talkie and I could only make out every other word. "Careful," I heard through the static.

"Elia," I whispered sharply as I got closer. "Elia! It's

Kat."

She was muttering to herself. Unintelligible words interspersed with what sounded like my name. I inched closer towards her, fingers reaching out to grasp her shoulder. *If I could just get her out of here, get back to the clearing, have Jay pull us out.*

My fingers touched her shoulder, just as her muttered words finally unjumbled and became clear.

"Curiosity killed the Kat."

She uncurled, then, and turned to look back at me. It was Elia's face, but her eyes were fathomless, completely black, not empty, filled with a vastness and an unending void so deep that it terrified me. It felt like looking at a moonless night sky. Instead of standing grounded on my backyard patio, I had stepped out beyond the sky, beyond the stars and planets, as if everything recognizable and warm was behind me and I was right on the edge where only the blackness remained. I stared at the vastness and it stared right back.

I snatched my hand back as if I'd been burned, and Elia slowly stood up to face me. She kept repeating the phrase, "curiosity killed the Kat," and as she straightened onto her feet, she cocked her head to the side, as if listening to something far off. Then, her head continued in that direction, bending further and further to the side, until I was sure her neck would snap, and it still kept going, turning around in a horrifying slow motion circle, those eyes staring at me, until her head had turned all the way around, and her chin pointed up towards the ceiling while her long hair dangled down the front of her body.

Her mouth opened wide, the sentient vastness of the abyss beyond the cavern of her mouth, and she screamed, multiple voices crying in an agony and rage that rocked me to my core.

I ran.

I have never felt such blinding terror before, or since. There was no reason, no plan, no strategy to where I was going. I simply threw myself forward into any available empty space that would take me, feet pounding against white wooden floorboards. I sprinted towards the front of the building. The Black Door slammed shut as I reached it, and I let out a strangled, helpless cry, trying the knob once before letting go, accepting that the door refused to budge. I turned and ran for the stairs, Elia's twisted, shuttering shape made its way toward me in a stuttering half-step.

I ran up the stairs, two steps at a time, legs and lungs burning, eyes watering, vision blurred. I heard a horrible, "crunch," as I reached the top of the stairs, and I turned to look behind me. Elia's form had reached the bottom step, and she had fallen forward, catching herself on her arms, limbs lengthening in horrible proportions as she began crawling up each step with unearthly speed. Her horribly turned head wobbling back and forth in grotesque fashion. Her mouth was still wide open, still screaming wordlessly.

I turned and sprinted down the dark hallway.

The ceiling was high, shadows stretching above me into nothingness. I threw myself around the corner at the end of the hall, only to find another stretch of hallway in front of me. With Elia close behind, I ran, further into the darkness, Elia's enraged screams echoing around me. The rumbling background sound had grown more intense, pulsating through me and vibrating my bones as I bounced off walls and skidded around corners, gasping for breath. No matter how many bursts of speed I put on, how many times I thought I'd lose her, she was soon on my trail again, crawling like some unearthly animal, long legs and arms stretching, snapping forward.

I glanced behind me, terror rising anew as I saw her skid around the corner I'd just cleared, and as my head turned, from the corner of my eye, I saw a glimpse of color.

A flash of deep red in the darkness.

To my right, down a side hallway, was the Red Door.

I should have questioned it, but there was no time. I hurtled towards it, Elia grabbing at my heels, and reached out for the doorknob, turning it in an instant and shoving it open. Light poured through the door, illuminating the hallway, and as I turned to slam the door shut, I caught a final glimpse of Elia. She was crawling on the ceiling, hands and feet gripping the darkened wood as her face, now right side up because of the angle, hung down, almost level with my own; her mouth split into a wicked grin.

"Curiousity killed the—"

I slammed the door shut, leaning against it hard.

*THUMP!* The door shook violently, rattling against my back. I squeezed my eyes shut and pressed harder against it, lips clamped together to stifle my own cries.

*Thump thump THUMP!*

*Go away, go away, go away…*

After a few moments, the door finally fell still. All sound from the other side ceased. I stood, drenched in sweat and gasping for breath, in the golden gilt courtyard we always entered when we stepped through the Red Door in the past. Impossibly tall buildings rose high above me, glittering in the light of a deep crimson sunset. The air was cooling, but the sparkling bricks and walls around me radiated the ambient heat of a long, hot day coming to a close.

"Jay," I said hoarsely. "Jay, can you hear me?"

"Yes! God, finally, are you okay? What's happening? You've been babbling nonsense and hyperventilating for the past five minutes. I was about to send someone to call 911."

"Jay. Elia… she's…"

A rush of hot wind tousled my hair, caressing my face. A shadow passed over the courtyard, and I quailed, looking up as a dark shape suddenly dropped down from the air, onto the cobbled pavement in front of me. An owl, huge, almost as tall as me, scrabbled its talons against the gilt stonework. It cocked its head at me once, twice, and then seemed to shiver, shake out its feathers, twitching uncomfortably.

Then a woman's head unfurled, standing tall, much taller than me, the feathers of the owl settling and draping over her body like a fine gown. She folded a pair of wings against her back; her eyes were impossibly large, nearly filled with luminescent red irises shot with gold, huge unchanging black pupils swallowing the middle.

"Kat... Kat, what is it? What do you see?"

Her crimson lips curled in a smile. Her voice was... otherworldly; intense. So uncanny that it raised the hairs on the back of my neck the moment she spoke.

"I've been waiting for you."

6

"Kat," Jay's voice whispered. "Kat, what do you see?"

"Give me a second," I whispered back. The woman paced in front of me; she seemed to have a hard time sitting completely still. While her eyes remained rapt and focused on me, her head shifted this way and that at every noise, tilting almost imperceptibly against the breeze. Her wings shifted and ruffled constantly, giving the impression of tireless energy, and intense power held at bay.

"You are younger than I expected," she said after a

moment. "Not yet a woman. But the smell of your blood is much older."

*Oh Jesus Christ, the smell of my blood???*

My knees nearly liquified; her presence was crushing, as if I was standing in front of every leader of every nation of earth. I was still pressed hard against the Red Door and refused to move forward into her wingspan. "I." I swallowed, clearing the sudden lump in my throat. "I apologize, um… but I don't know what that means."

She seemed to find that funny. "You are truly a youngling. And yet you and the others wander through these expanses with such relative ease. We have watched you ever since you stepped through that door." Her gaze snapped to the Red Door behind my back, and then back down to my face, obvious interest unveiled on her features. "You have something that would be very valuable to many here."

I didn't know what to say to that. I opened my mouth to ask what she meant, but she suddenly cocked her head sharply to the side, pupils contracting to tiny pinpoints of black in a sea of red and gold. "It encroaches. Whatever you've done to disturb It, It now presses Its influence between the expanses." Her gaze flicked back to me. "You are here to clean up your missteps, yes?"

"I… um. Yes. That's the goal." I felt like I had forgotten something extremely important when talking to her; as if she were in on an inside joke that she expected me to join her in, and yet I didn't know what it was.

"It's coming closer." She shook her head, feathers ruffling around her face for a moment, and her wings expanded. "It may know that you are here. I tire of holding this form, but I will give you this: that Its door and Its Self are intrinsically connected. It is a being of gateways, of passages, of in-betweens and not-places. What you do to Its gateway, you do to Its Self."

She shuddered before I could get a word out, shivered and hunched forward, and in an undulating ripple of feathers, the woman was gone and the owl blinked at me, wickedly hooked beak flashing in the eternal sunset. It flapped its wings in a powerful down beat and lifted off the ground, rising higher overhead before clearing the skyline of buildings and disappearing, taking off into the twilight.

"Jay," I said quietly when she was gone. "I think I have an idea."

"What happened?"

"I'll tell you, I promise, but just bear with me. I may not be able to talk much."

I took off in a light run, keeping my eyes peeled for anything that would seem out of place in the red-gold world. Every few moments, a shadow would fall across me as a dark shape would fly overhead between buildings; like every time before when we had explored the world behind the Red Door, I was watched from a distance. I wondered

235

if it were only the owl woman watching, or if there were more like her far above me in the sky.

And then, as I reached a wide open marketplace, empty of stalls or beings, I heard it.

A low rumbling, with a choppier sound layered over the top.

*Fuck.*

"It's here, Jay. I don't have much time." I walked out to the center of the empty marketplace, turning in a slow circle, watching the nearby buildings and doors. "When I say so, I need everyone in the circle, including you, to picture the Green Door in your minds. Try not to think of anything else, but just the Green Door. You got it?"

"Okay, we can do that. What are you doing?"

"Right now? I'm waiting."

The noise grew. Not louder, but intensified—sending low vibrations throughout my body. The gilt cobblestone beneath my feet seemed to shiver through the bottoms of my shoes, and I kept turning, barely blinking, staring hard into the surrounding architecture. On my third turn in this manner, I saw it.

The Black Door.

"All right," I said quietly. "If I die, or go crazy, you guys had better come in and fix this."

"No promises," Jay said wryly; I could sense her attempt at humor, but underneath her voice, there was a slight tremble. She was scared.

*That made two of us.*

I walked slowly towards the door. It looked the same as it had before, but larger, looming against the backdrop of a glittering, golden wall set on the far end of the marketplace. I was a tall girl, and the door knob was almost as high as my eye level, making me feel like a child again. I turned it, and purposefully pulled the door open.

The inside of a barn greeted me, heavily obscured in shadows, dead straw and dirt scattering into the darkness ahead of me.

I took a deep breath, and stepped through. The moment I crossed the threshold, I was once again in the gray world; color gone and that distant noise thrumming through my bones.

But this time, I turned, and immediately shut the door behind me. "Jay," I whispered. "Now. Now, now, now, do it, the Green Door."

"Come on you guys," I heard Jay say; her voice was muffled and far away, but I heard her, and with that, I pushed the Black Door back open. The red world was gone, and in front of me were the blanched, gray woods, so similar and yet so different from the woods we had created ourselves.

I stepped back outside, heading purposefully into the forest.

I had taken a few steps when I heard a deep, heavy thrumming, and glanced over my shoulder back towards the barn.

It stood there, in front of the Black Door. It was tall, much taller than the threshold of the door, and roughly humanoid shaped, but dark, like a hole had opened up in the world and had taken on sentient form. The edges of Its shape seemed to bend and warp the atmosphere immediately around it. As I stared, the darkness seemed to deepen, and I thought I began catching glimpses of something else. Far behind in the blackness, there began to appear the hints of a shape, or shapes. Shapes with extra edges, with lines and dips and points in places that made no sense, undulating in unsettling movement when my eyes looked elsewhere. My stomach churned in repulsion, my eyes desperately wanting to reject what I was seeing.

I felt a trickle of wetness slide down my cheek as I stared, and I reached up to wipe my eyes; my fingers coming away stained with blood. My head was pounding. My very thoughts squeezing under Its heavy weight, and as I stepped back, It seemed to take a step towards me.

And then another.

*Fuck no.* I turned and ran, hurtling into the trees.

"Jay!" I cried. "Come on you guys! I need that Green Door!"

She didn't answer. The forest around me kept flickering, shifting in a cacophony of buzzing noises and that deep rumbling sound. Trees were to my left or right in one moment and then suddenly in front of me in the next, and I had to keep changing my direction; a few times I slammed into tree trunks, scrabbling in a panic against the ground as I regained my footing. I glanced behind me a few times, and always, the shadow followed, seeming to never lose ground, but always gaining a little, following steadily behind me, long limbs moving in disquieting non-synchronicity, with the patience and dark purpose of something that has all the time in the world.

I felt myself weakening. It was different from getting tired in the physical world. I suddenly felt less, as if I were a canister of water that had cracked, and was slowly spilling my contents out onto the ground around me. My vision began blurring, tunneling at the edges. Nausea overtook me, and I was panting heavily, sweat and a darker liquid sliding down the sides of my face and into my eyes. Its thrumming, deep, bone cracking sound sunk into my body and I could feel it squeezing, pressing, emptying.

"Jay," I whispered weakly, and tripped over a tree root that had suddenly appeared in my path. I hit the ground hard, breath escaping my lungs in a heavy grunt, and I turned onto my back as the shadow closed in on me, reaching ever taller in the sky, Its edges rippling like the surface of a puddle that had begun to spread.

"Jay!" I scrabbled backwards, and then my hands touched something underneath me, something that felt wholly alien compared to the pine needle covered ground.

Smooth, solid wood, and the shape of a door knob.

I glanced down. The Green Door had appeared directly underneath my body, lying on the ground. I didn't hesitate, but gripped the knob hard and turned it, allowing the door to fall open beneath my body. I flew downwards, my brain spinning at the shift in orientation, and I landed heavily on the sandy shore of the grotto, sprawling with the Green Door open in the cave wall in front of me.

I could see the gray sky through the door, and as I scrambled to my feet. The dark shadow bent down over the door, blocking out the sky, filling the opening as It tried to reach through. I swiftly leapt forward, grabbed the edge of the door, and slammed it shut in Its face.

I held it closed for a moment, panting. "If you want me, asshole," I whispered, "You'll have to come in here the hard way."

I turned and faced the grotto. It was exactly as we had left it: gorgeous. Luminescent algae made the water glow, while threads of fungus wove a tapestry of green, blue, and purple across the rock walls. The far edge of the underground cavern opened up into landscape and sky far above, but what I focused on now was the little camp that had always been at the edge of the water. The tent, and the campfire blazing merrily away in a fire pit dug in the sand.

I moved quickly. I knew It would have an easier time pressing into the expanse this time, and I swiftly knocked over the tent, stepping hard on the fabric and pulling up with all my strength, ripping it open. I removed one of the tent poles, and snapped it in a similar way, using my weight to bend and break the flexible wood. I quickly bound the shattered pieces together with the shredded tent canvas, and repeated this a few times, until I had at least four bundles of wood bound in cloth.

A deep rumbling filled the air. *Whop whop whop whop…*

I turned to face the far cavern wall. In the space of a blink, there was smooth rock wall, and then the Black Door was there, ominous in its height, a black stain in this beautiful place. I moved fast, my heart pounding; no time to question or quail.

I grabbed one end of one of the bundles and passed the other end through the campfire; it took a few tries, but soon the thick wood and bundled fabric caught fire. I looked up as I straightened, and noticed that this time, It wasn't waiting for me; the door had begun slowly swinging outwards on its own.

I approached it quickly, and as it swung open, there It was, standing in a far off field of gray grass, a stark black wound against the sky, tall and impossible. It began walking towards me. I held my breath, swung my arms back with all my strength, and tossed the flaming bundle through the door.

The last thing I saw through the door was an eruption of white, colorless flame as the bundle landed in that dry sea of dead grass and immediately caught fire.

My eardrums nearly burst at the explosion of sound

that reverberated from that fathomless thing filled the air with sound. I gripped the edge of the Black Door and shoved it closed with all my strength.

I wasn't done yet. Two more bundles went against the base of the door, and I lit a third bundle on fire just as I had done the first bundle. With my flaming prize in hand, I stalked towards the Black Door.

*THUMP!*

It rattled and shook. The knob turned furiously back and forth.

I carefully bent down and placed the flaming bundle against the others, propping it up so that the fire would have a stable base.

*THUNK!*

I lunged back. The door bowed outward, an unearthly rumbling filling the cavern for a moment, wood screeching in protest, and then the fire caught and blazed stronger and stronger, finding purchase in the kindling I had provided, and began to steadily work its way up the surface of the Black Door.

A horrible keening ripped through the grotto, and I slammed my hands over my ears, falling to my knees. Rock cracked, and split, dust and pebbles falling to the sandy grotto floor, and I curled down into a ball, eyes squeezed shut, waiting for the worst.

And then the rumbling slowly went silent.

I looked up. I was a lone girl kneeling in a grotto,

watching a slowly growing fire blaze merrily away.

I moved and sat at the far end, pressing myself against the cave wall next to the Green Door, and watched it burn all the way down, wanting to make sure. While I sat, I related to Jay and the others what had occurred in the red world, and how I used the campfire in the grotto to hopefully destroy the Black Door. I waited, ready to run if my plan didn't seem to work, but as I watched, the flames seemed to burn brighter and brighter, until the door finally crumbled in a heaping pile of ash and coals, leaving nothing but a smooth, rock wall behind it.

I stood, turned to the Green Door, and cautiously opened it.

Lush, green woods greeted me. I stepped through, closing the door behind me. I could feel my weariness digging through my mind as I trekked back through the forest, heading in the direction of our all-too-familiar clearing. On the way, I spotted some movement far off between the trees; as I glanced to my left, a beast very similar to an elk, but larger, with dark-tipped horns and a large, staring eye in the middle of its sable forehead, caught my gaze. It inclined its head to the side for a moment, before turning and disappearing into the forest.

When I reached the clearing, Elia was there, waiting.

I stopped, eyeing her cautiously. She looked like her normal self, wearing the pajamas she had worn Friday night.

"Are you actually you?" I asked.

She snorted at me. "Do you have any idea what I just went through? Don't be a dick."

*Well, it definitely sounded like Elia.*

I walked into the clearing, eyeing her warily. She was not a demonstrative person, but she smiled at me as I approached. "Not bad," she said. "Thanks for coming back." She took my hand.

It would have been easy in that moment to mistrust everything I had been seeing, but a part of me needed to believe that we had fixed whatever it was that we had broken.

"Jay," I said, "Bring us back." I squeezed Elia's hand and closed my eyes.

"Five, four, three, two, one… open your eyes!"

\*\*\*

Elia was back in school the next day. She seemed pale, and still a little weak, but mostly herself. She said she didn't remember much while she was sick, and was constantly in and out of consciousness with a bad fever. She didn't remember anything about the part of herself that was lost in the shadow land's gray world, or coming back with me, but didn't seem overly concerned about it. I think she was just relieved that she wasn't sick anymore, and was eager to put it all behind her. All of us were.

We never went out into the woods again, and once high school came around, we all seemed to drift and go our separate ways. I've lost touch with most of my old friends through the years. Some I've found again on Facebook, and a few I saw at my high school reunion a few years ago. Everyone seems to be well adjusted in their adulthood, but no one has ever tried anything like Seven Doors again.

No one seems to have any contact with Elia, or know where she is.

I've mostly stayed away from any sort of astral projection, lucid dreaming exercises, or journeying type meditations. While I tend toward being agnostic and skeptical, I also collect various religious paraphernalia, including blessed St. Benedictine amulets. One I keep in the house, the other in my car. I also have a few statues of saints and Vedic deities. Ganesha guards the hallway upstairs in my house.

We have little Jizo statues on the front porch, and sometimes I surreptitiously hide little bowls of salt in the corners of the house. My husband thinks it's quirky, that I am constantly questioning everything and demanding proof, but then secretly filling the house with protective charms and statues.

Last year, I became pregnant with my first child. I found that I was having increasingly vivid dreams, which is common during pregnancy, but something strange about them made me question what I was really dreaming, and made me think back on this childhood experience. A couple of times, I would dream that I was walking through beautifully sunlit woods, relaxed and comfortable, and though he didn't show up physically as himself, I could feel the presence of my child with me, floating over my shoulder like a tiny ball of warmth. We would walk for what seemed like hours, taking in the woods. Sometimes never speaking, but feeling each other deeply in a way that I can't really describe. If you've ever carried or given birth to children, you may know what I mean.

During one of these dreams, I remember sitting at the edge of a pond, looking out across the expanse of water, the little presence of my son hovering softly next to me. For some reason, I looked down into the water below me, admiring the reflection of the woods in the still, smooth surface. I saw something strange on the far end of the pond, reflected back in the water. Puzzled, I glanced up.

Ahead of me, across the water, a large gray barn stood on the shoreline. The barn was on fire.

Alarm and a sudden shock of terror shot through me, and I gasped awake, shaking. My husband woke up, asked me if I was alright, and did his best to settle me down before falling back asleep.

I don't knowingly enter any sort of meditation that may take me elsewhere. After that experience, I know better. Maybe we stopped It for a little while; made Its connection to whatever plane we were exploring a little weaker. But I know that what we did won't last, that I am not forgotten, and that I am still, twenty years later, being watched. Maybe, someday, I'll find a way of severing Its connection to me for good.

Be safe, travelers.

And for fuck's sake, if you see it, please never open a Black Door.

# Please Read; I Need You

## By fromwarwick

---

I apologize ahead of time. I am sorry, so sorry, reader. I've been urged to open up, to share my experience, as I've no conscious connections left in the waking world. I know that at this point, I'm just a no-face person, but I need to share this with someone. Anyone.

Besides the hospice worker that comes to the house, my only other companion lies unconscious in my living room. He means everything to me. If he passes, I'm not sure what will happen to me. There is no way for me to ready myself for such a loss. I feel so alone.

His body speaks to me in the hush and huff of his breathing machines; an occasional mechanical signal breaks the silence. We only have each other now, and I am thankful that I can still slip my hand in his, rest my head against his chest and listen to his heart thump out: *I'm still here, I'm still here.*

I need a hug right now, I need so many things.

Here's my story. Please take some time out of your day to read it—to absorb it into you.

xx Brenna

***

It wasn't always like this. Before Brant came into my life—conscious and normal, mind you—I was surrounded by general loneliness. At first, I considered myself an outcast; I repelled most people like a magnet. It was an easy thing to do. My mother believed in geographical cures for her emotional ailments, and having the constant stigma as "new kid" made it hard for me to form strong friendships.

But the more we moved, the more I realized I was like a domino architect. Instead of repelling potential friends, I had the misfortune of setting up events to push everyone away from me. They'd all fallen away by the time I met Brant.

My father was my first casualty. I couldn't help it. Born a Daddy's girl. One of the rare times my mother sat up to talk with me, she told me how smitten he was with my newborn dark curls, the laughter in my eyes as I gurgled and reached for him. Fatherhood a mantle that he proudly wore. Before me, he practiced law with my mother at a small and successful firm in the city. Always the more competitive one, the career driven one, it was a surprise to my mother, and the firm, when he put it all on hold when I was born.

So my mother worked, and my father raised me. For my first few years, we had an idyllic family. Mother would work long into the night, and Father would look after me and lead me into childhood. He'd tuck polaroids of me into Mother's lunches, and she had clusters of them all over her office. Our two, smiling faces.

He'd homeschooled me through elementary school, taking me on road trips across the country. Showing me history, teaching me geometry through pool, astronomy through a lens, geology digging through the mud; we adventured. He was my whole world, my closest friend.

When Father got sick, my Mother took it hard. To his credit, he'd hid it from her for a couple years. Maybe himself, too. Sickness sneaks up on you like that sometimes. You feel more tired than usual, and then weaker, and we can easily attribute it to getting older, to the albatrosses hung around our necks. Being a parent is hard. So he put me first. Always. I guess until the end.

Then he passed away, and it was just the two of us, and the polaroids. Mother had given me the stacks and stacks of photographs from her office. She kept a picture of just the two of them in a small frame on her desk from when they first started dating. They'd gone to a photo booth on their second or third date, and he'd kissed her in the last photograph. The thin little frame protected their unlined faces smiling and carefree, those moments lost to long ago.

As a child, I knew Mother wasn't handling his loss well. Instead of taking a step back from trying to make partner at the law firm, she worked harder than ever and was rarely home. In her place, she provided me with an endless swarm of nannies. She made sure her little girl was well provided for.

I had a few memorable ones that had stayed. Gerta with her shock of red hair and her ability to always have hot honeyed rolls for breakfast, Sonya and her perfect eyebrows and patient hands teaching me to crochet, Maddie and her little girl that played dolls with me endlessly. Some nannies stayed longer than others, but just as I connected with them, a new one would take her place.

My nanny was a transient role that was filled until I was in high school, Mother moved us when a better opportunity arose for her, and it meant I rarely had enough time to put down roots or grow attachments in an area. I have pictures of all of them, pictures and memories and it still draws tears to my eyes to think of all of those goodbyes.

My nannies did what they could for me so I could grow up into a strong young woman. I felt like many of them tried to fill that motherly role. To this day, I'm so grateful to have had so many women that I could look up to and grow from. Without them, I'm not sure if I'd be here today.

I was in ninth grade when my Mother deemed me too old for a nanny, and had given me the honor of autonomy. The bus route picked me up at home and dropped me off promptly at the same time every day. Once home, I knew how to prepare dinner, and then would set about my routine of cleaning and doing homework. I'd spent a lot of my free time reading, or crocheting and watching television. Characters created in print and screen staved off a bit of that longing for companionship.

This is around the time the dreams started, whenever I felt lonely lonely. Being so isolated, you get this hunger for social interaction kind of like the feeling of when you miss breakfast. It's there, drumming away behind your eyes and as long as you're focused and doing something you won't notice. Everybody dreams, every night. We mostly don't remember our dreams, but for those that do dreams range from the ridiculous, to the comforting, to terrifying.

As a girl, who lived mostly alone, I started looking forward to my dreams. Sometimes, Father would be there and we'd do things like fly over the mountains in Colorado and the red oaks in Oregon as if the states were stitched side by side. We'd sit on the Presidential noses of Mount Rushmore. Sometimes I'd dream that, while cleaning, I'd find new and hidden rooms in my house, and Father lived in there.

The kitchen pantry would have a false panel and I would be able to crush my body in such a way to find a new hallway that smelled like him. My bare feet could feel the dusty floorboards as I found his room and his study in our first house. I'd wake elated and ready to launch out of bed to tell Mother; only to find my cheeks wet to realize that I'd been dreaming. There was no fake panel in the pantry. Father was gone; I was alone.

Then I'd dream of my nannies, taking me home. Of Sonya and her crochet hook, weaving me a perfect blanket in blues, greens, and purples as we sipped hot chocolate by the fire with a record on. Gerta would take me up in her arms and declare me her best friend, I'd never had one before, and we'd go over my rock collection—touching each one as I recounted its story. Maddie and the little girl would hold my hand and take me into the garden, and we'd make floral crowns with wildflowers and weeds. We'd thrown stones in a still lake, and stained our mouths with fresh blackberries to the baritone choir of frogs.

And every morning I'd wake up alone. I packed my lunch, brushed my hair, donned my jumper, and took the bus to school. At school, the buzz of teens around me made me feel even more alone. Forming friendships wasn't as easy as it was when I dreamed.

I tried. I formed weak acquaintances that let me sit with them at lunch. As a good student, I never suffered to find a group to work with for projects, and I bore my meager athleticism well when I grouped with others during gym. Occasionally, I'd be invited to birthday parties. I'd eat cake, and enjoy hanging out with other people my age, but I always felt like an outsider or an addition.

I wasn't generally bullied, or picked on, mind you, but I wasn't liked enough to form ready friendships where I could just call someone up from a memorized phone number. Girls would either not have room in their friend circles, or I didn't live in any one place long enough to find my way into one. I could get people talk to me, but I could never get them to listen to me, to make a connection. The friendships were one sided. I couldn't help but feel like a fisherman that religiously got his bait stolen, and went home with a sunburn and no supper. During summer months, we'd either move, or I'd explore my neighborhood alone. And I kept looking forward to my dreams.

In tenth grade hit, I started having a reoccurring dream. I'd wake up on a swell of a hill. A sycamore tree bent over the surface of a smooth lake, and an older woman with short hair cropped just below her chin, smiling.

"Welcome home, Brenna!"

In the dream, I'd run out to her, and hug her waist. The dreams had started before my growth spurt, and the woman was tall and warm. It felt safe to press my face into her apron, to have my little frame engulfed in her arms.

She'd pet me, and say pretty things to me that I wished my mother would tell me. My face would contort and I'd hold back tears when she would tell me how proud of me she was.

She had a son that was a couple years older than me, and we'd play. He had a tree house, and we'd eat lunches, play card games, and decorate the tree house with things we found by the lake. A built-in shelf housed a squirrel skull we found in the mud at the base of a tree, a limestone rock with a million fossilized shells, and piece of green glass worn smooth by water and time.

These two people in the reoccurring dream would remember what I told them. As the seasons changed in my life, theirs did, too. In every way it felt real, except for the slight detail that from their noses up their faces were in shadow. In the dream, I didn't notice, but upon waking it felt like those two people could be anyone. The boy had a small blunt chin, brown curls, and round cheeks. He was a little gangly, but I didn't mind. Even in my dreams I ran awkwardly with the grace of a three legged grasshopper.

I also didn't know his name, or his mother's name—details that washed away upon waking. As my mother and I hopped from state to state, I stopped caring that she was rarely home when I was awake. I stopped caring that I didn't have friends. I got to see my friends every night for eight hours.

At the time, I didn't think it was abnormal to have

reoccurring dreams nearly every night. My friendship with the boy, as he turned into a man, changed as I got older. In a few years, we'd hold each other in the tree house, and I'd bury my face in his chest and he'd rest his cheek on the top of my head. We grew close, and I felt differently for him, more for him, each time I woke.

His mother would give me a knowing look and laugh when I'd wake up there, and I'd blush and find him. Friends didn't hold hands the way we held hands, as we looked over the lake and listened to wave after wave of crickets chirping and the reflection of thousands of fireflies blinking in and out like far off star light.

It wasn't until I was a senior in high school that I found out that my dreams were abnormal. In a creative writing class, we were prompted to write on our most memorable dream. Easily, I filled pages and pages on my sleeping life. I wrote of how last night, we'd been soaking our feet in the lake off a worn pier, my cuffed jeans skimmed the water and we tried to stay still enough to let the minnows nibble at our toes. In the reflection of the water, I saw his face break out into a broad brace-faced grin. Then he tickled me.

Even though I saw him coming, I couldn't help but curl and writhe in my fit of laughter, rolling into his lap and gripping onto him, ultimately thrashing us both into the water. The dream ended when he kissed the top of my forehead and temple and then patted his cheek twice with two fingers. It was our ritual. I reached up on the tips of my toes and kissed him twice on the same cheek. A kiss for now, and another when you need it later.

I sat in class and listened as everyone read out loud their dreams. One girl read out, "I don't usually remember my dreams. I mean, like, if I do it's just a fragment of something. Last night I dreamt that someone had broken in, and I was trying to get my dad. Suddenly the burglar was right behind me, and I felt him there, you know? And no matter how fast I'd run, he was faster. It was like my legs wouldn't work. I was so scared, I woke up right before I could feel his hands around my neck. I couldn't get back to sleep. Nightmares suck."

"I dreamt that I'd been playing football with my team, you know. Everything was normal, except the mascot was a real tiger and we could jump like Master Chief in Halo. Man, I wish that were real life. Tigers are cool," a boy exclaimed, miming throwing a football.

A girl blushed and demurely tucked a stray hair behind her ear, "I, uh, dreamt that The Doctor came to take me away. Ten, as in David Tennant. I got to go into the Tardis, and I got to see the pool! Yeah, I wish I'd have that one every night."

Then it was my turn. I briefly explained that I generally dreamed every night and a few of the other details.

Tardis girl spoke up, first, "Maybe that's like your

soulmate?"

"I've never had the same dream twice, that's weird," football boy laughed.

"It must be nice to dream every night. That sounds nice," the girl with the nightmare said. She smiled at me.

The class suggested all sorts of things: see a medium, look up dream meanings, post a classified ad to find my soulmate, and to keep a dream journal before the end bell broke us up. It left me a little befuddled and curious for the first time as to the significance of the dreams.

For all my life, I'd felt an overwhelming urge to connect with people. Dreams are not enough to sustain a person, and I felt tired. I had always wanted the dreams to be meaningful. Really, I assumed that they were. Mother was working overseas by then, and while she supported me diligently, life was a vacuum.

The rational side of my being decided that I should talk to someone. It wasn't normal for an eighteen year old to have no friends, an absent mother, a dead father, and a dream boyfriend. It couldn't be healthy. Sure, many other teens had it worse. My family wasn't abusive, and my mother had made sure I felt provided for. We didn't have to worry about money, and I was spoiled insofar that if I wanted something, I could just buy it. By the time I was in high school, I had my own small library at home. Still, with no one to talk to, I started talking to my school's counselor, Mr. Goldstein as a last resort.

He assured me that he'd seen my type before. Kids that had trouble fitting in, kids that moved and had their roots pulled out so many times that it stunted their emotional growth. He tried his best to be helpful. Whenever I felt morose, he'd listen. When I told him of my troubles concerning friendships, he'd suggested extracurricular clubs, after school activities, hobbies. I really poured myself out to him, and it had been ages since I'd had someone really listen to me. My nannies were the last people that I had such ties with, and all I had left of them were my memories, I didn't dream of them anymore.

Then, as everyone had, Mr. Goldstein left, too. The school told me he had to take a leave of absence for personal reasons. It happened from time to time. Adults have tons of obligations, and I was passed onto his replacement, Ms. Kwan. I liked her well enough, but I felt as though she wasn't as invested. It felt almost like going to the doctor rather than opening up to a potential friend. Even with Mr. Goldstein gone, he gave me the push to ready myself for graduation and to apply for colleges. It would have to be enough.

Mother decided to stay overseas, and to sell our home. She bought me a condo in the northeast next to a large university I was accepted into. Driven to succeed and provide, Mother gave me a generous stipend every month. Even though she couldn't be there for me physically, she made sure I had the means to survive. As always.

Once again in a different part of the country, and new school, I set out to find a piece of normalcy. Still, I dreamed of my boy and his lake. His braces were gone, and he was substantially taller than me. His shoulders were broad, and his chin and cheeks had started sporting thatches of dark bristles. His lips still carried the flush fullness that he had as a boy, and I enjoyed kissing them all night. It was my favorite hobby. It was a good thing he wasn't real, or else I might have not taken my studies seriously.

I had decided on library sciences, but I had to make it through my first two years at university before I started in on my major. College felt more isolating than high school. New classes brought in tides of new faces and I had still not found the skill to make fast friends; or slow friends, to be honest. I was in my junior year of college when I started feeling tired. It started with oversleeping and I attributed it to wanting to spend more time with my nocturnal other world, but as sleeping into late morning ate into early afternoon, I started to worry.

I was getting more hungry too, but even though I started eating more, I started to lose weight. My nightly walks started to get tiresome more quickly, and I found it hard to walk up the stairs. I was so exhausted some nights. In my dreams, my boyfriend urged me to go see a doctor. He told me I looked more pale than usual, that my hands shook. My mother told me that a true summer vacation may be what I needed, and she encouraged me to take a trip. To fly out to more familiar grounds.

I took the boy's advice first and scheduled an appointment with my doctor. He poked and prodded me, checked my thyroid and ran several tests on my blood work and heart. Besides having slightly below normal iron levels, he could find nothing wrong with me. He suspected that it may be stress related and encouraged my mother's suggestion for a vacation.

I found a short lease to a furnished house in the City where I was born, and flew out there to have a new perspective over the summer. Even though I'd moved a half a dozen or so times since my father passed, it never got easier. Each move was draining, and at the end of each year I started feeling an aching anxiety when I had to fill up my boxes. Simply attending the same college for three full years was strangely sweet. Despite being able to get used to the same walls, and form a fondness for the routes where I would walk, I didn't feel sad leaving my condo for the summer. In my hometown, I had found a favorite coffee spot, next to the library, and I'd often spend a quiet chunk of my day stopping at each favorite place on my personal pilgrimage.

Every day for that first month, I'd leave the house, walk the couple miles to the library, pick out a new book to read, and then take breakfast, lunch, and liberal amounts of coffee at the café. I'd eye up an orange scone and an iced coffee and often see right through the person who took my order. I'd grown so used to not being seen, that I had stopped seeing people. So I took my copy of Jane Eyre, my breakfast, and I sat out in the sun and let the literature and sun warm my body and soul.

That night, in my sleeping world, I enjoyed my time with my boyfriend. His mother had made us cold turkey sandwiches and packed us a liter of cold Coke and we munched on the offerings with our feet splashing in the cold lake water. He took a bite of his sandwich and looked over at me, slipping a dark curl between his fingers, "Are you real?" I could feel his eyes looking at me, touching on the sharp and soft features on my face.

I laughed, we avoided this conversation. We'd just never had it. In all the years I visited him, I was happy to have a place where I was normal. I didn't want my afflictions to invade this part, this comfort, "What kind of question is that? Of course I'm real. I think I'm more real, here with you, than I am when I wake up."

He blinked. In this world I could both see and not see his face. It was like that experience of deja vu when I woke up, the memory of his face was somewhere.

"You wake up? Brenna, you dream all of this, too?" he became still, and I felt disorientated with the realization that I'd hoped for this. I'd hoped that I were special; I'd hoped that dreams could be real, and that connections made with people were not only through flesh and bone.

"Yes. I go to sleep, I dream of you and your mom, and I wake up in my own bed. I remember most things, and pretty much I have the same dream with you, here," my heart skittered like a rabbit that wanted to run. The textures of my dream were almost a form of hyper realism, and I could hear the trees and their leaves kissing the wind, the lake water smelled like wet moss and silt, and held my sandwich lamely. It was soggy.

"Am I crazy? We're dreaming. This isn't real. You're not real. You're some figment of my imagination drummed up to fulfill some sort of loneliness that I felt. It can't be healthy, I look forward to these dreams, I look forward to seeing you and mom again, to this damn cabin. Brenna, I think I even see you. I think I see you when I'm awake, I—" he put his face in his hands and shuddered. I put my hand on his back and tried to calm him and silently wondered if he could feel my heart beating out of my chest.

"You know, I think those things, too. I haven't seen you in… the real world, at least I don't think, I don't remember what you look like, it's vague," I frowned and let my cool forehead rest on his bare shoulder.

"You think you saw me?"

"Yeah. Where I work. You come in and order an orange scone and an iced coffee every day and read. It was your smile," I froze and stopped rubbing his back and we straightened and our eyes met. Truly met. "Brenna, what

264

book were you reading?"

"Jane Eyre. I just picked up a copy of Jane Eyre."

The next day, I met Brant. He wasn't working, he'd called off and he was sitting at a table looking at the door nervously. I had my copy of Jane Eyre tucked under my arm and I nearly dropped it when I saw him.

That's when my life really started.

Brant told me about his life, and I told him about mine. His mother had died when he was in middle school. It was a freak accident, they'd been up in their cabin in the U.P. and he and his dad were out fishing when it happened. His mom was eating breakfast by herself and choked and died. They found her on the floor in the middle of the afternoon, and it was far too late.

For Brant, his childhood ended there. They buried his mom, sold the vacation home, and Brant kind of lost his father, too. His father was there, but he'd never gotten over his wife's death. He'd taken up drinking, and they were barely getting by. Brant worked as a manager at the local café to help. He started dreaming of his mom when he had a bad day, and then one day I showed up.

He had a more normal life than I had lived. He had a good group of friends, and had even tried dating a girl in high school. Although, he said, that things never felt right. They didn't click as easily as we did, and for the longest time he thought he was being unfair, comparing her to a dream—a ghost. But between going to college and working, he found himself in a better place  as a single guy.

That's how things began. It was beautiful. I started feeling better. Before bed, each night, we'd chat over web cam and we'd share our days. At night, we still shared dreams; except now, the settings would change from time to time. Brant sometimes appeared in my childhood home, or at a beloved travel destination I visited in my youth. While we were still long distance, we spent hours together.

I finished up and got my degree, and moved back to my home town. We bought a little condo, and helped out his dad, got him into some programs to try and settle his demons. We felt so lucky, and I felt so normal. He proposed, and we started talking about having a family together. I bought a couple onesies, one for a girl and one for a boy, and laid them side by side imagining the little body that could fill it.

Then he got sick. It started with him being tired all the time, he started losing weight, his hands started shaking and he got so weak. Just like what happened to me. The doctors tried to find out what was wrong with him, and all the tests they performed came back normal. He was normal, but he was wasting away. His body started shutting down, and he was put into hospice care. My care.

He was no longer in my dreams. But I had the man, his body, this shell, and I could hold its hand. I've never felt so alone. They say it is better to have loved and lost than to have never loved at all; without him I would live half a life. I knew what it meant to be happy, and without Brant that happiness would be lost. Doctors could not help him, medicine did nothing, love only gave him comfort, so I resorted to the last thing I could think of.

I hired a medium.

Did you know you can find them in the yellow pages? She came to our condo, in a beat up old gremlin. She had no bag, no talismans, no show. Madame Celeste was a fair woman, with skin that looked like she was in her twenties and hair that was aging into her fifties. She'd seen sun, and freckles dotted her nose where her brown rimmed glasses rested. She fit the flare of medium with a sort of boho chic style, and I thoroughly believed I would have been better burning my money rather than calling her.

"Can I see the man?" she stood in our hallway. At least she was direct. I nodded and led her into our bedroom where he was set up. She pulled a chair to his bed and touched the air around him. She touched his face lightly, laid her hands slightly above his chest, and then settled with just holding his hand, closing her eyes. She frowned.

"He's still there. Vaguely. He's almost gone."

"Gone? Is he dying?" I blinked rapidly. I didn't need a medium to tell me Brant was fading. He was nearly a skeleton with skin. The physical evidence made that apparent.

"Dying? Yes. If he leaves, he will die. His, essence,

spirit, soul, what have you, is almost gone. He's nearly empty. So empty, this one," she looked perplexed.

"What does that mean? He's empty? His... soul is missing?" I didn't have words. This was insane. The woman, insane.

"There are multiple kinds of death. Naturally, our bodies house our spirits until it breaks down. Like any building, time takes its toll. Then the spirit moves on, as is the natural order of things. But the body needs a soul, just like a soul needs a body. This body's soul is very damaged. Just scraps of it left. I don't know what's causing it, but he could repair if no more damage is done. You can have hope," she looked at me. Looked through me. "Can I take your hand?"

I nodded, and gave the woman my hand. Hers were cool and smooth, and mine were sweaty and shaking. She took a moment and closed her eyes, a line forming between her brows, her eyes snapped open and she dropped her hand.

"Leave here. Leave here now if you love him. Call your mother. She has what you must know, I must go," she stood up, and shook herself, casting a bewildered look between Brant and me.

I blinked, confused, afraid, "What does that mean? Leave? Why? Why do I have to go, why should I call my mother?"

She swallowed, "She knows things you have not seen,

have not accepted. It is not my place to tell you, but she knows why, she's known all this time. She knows what went wrong. Good bye, Ms. Brenna." And she left. I tried to go after her, but she ignored me mutely, got in her beat up car, and, with a sputter, drove off. I tried to call her. I tried to find her business, but she would not give me anything else.

I called my Mother. She sent me letters from time to time. Emails to make sure I was all right, to check in on Brant. We weren't close, we'd never been close. She always had her work, and overseas she found a life she couldn't have in this country. I'd forgiven her a long time ago.

The phone rang, and within a few seconds she picked up, "Brenna? Are you all right? Why are you calling? It's late." Ah, yes. The time difference, I forgot. The sudden phone call mixed with the abruptness of the call must have startled her. I told her what had happened that day, awkwardly. I felt so foolish. I never told her about my day, or my life, or the petty little things that bothered me. She was always too busy, her time too valuable for me to waste on my little problems.

She remained silent as I finished, and sucked in a breath, "Brenna. Dear. I'm sorry, I'm so, so sorry." She started crying. I've never heard my mother cry.

"Your father and I were so in love and we desperately wanted children. We tried for years. We tried IVF. We tried fertility treatments. There was something wrong with

269

me, I couldn't have children. Sweetheart, I desperately wanted to be a mother. I wanted to have my own child, I wanted to have a child that was a product of our love and I was so selfish and stupid," she shuddered as she cried and talked.

"I prayed every night for a miracle. One night, I had a dream at a crossroad. There just me, and a well dressed man. He told me he had heard of my difficulty, and that he wanted to help. That I could help him, too, and that there would be no price that I would have to pay. I agreed, Brenna, he was so nice and comforting. It was such a nice dream to be freely given the life I so desperately wanted. So I accepted. And then you were born—my miracle baby.

"You were perfect, with a crown of dark curls and you couldn't stop smiling. Your father was even more enamored with you than I was, and begged me to stay home to raise you. So he stayed home and took care of you, for your every need and want, and we were so happy. You remember?"

I nodded, holding back tears. My father was my whole world back then, he tried so hard to be a good father, "Yes, Mother."

"Then he got sick. At first he was just tired, then he started to lose weight, his hands started to shake, and he got so weak. One day he just collapsed, and then couldn't get out of bed. The doctors couldn't figure out what happened. They couldn't figure out why he was so sick, his blood tests, his MRI, everything: normal," my heart stopped. I never heard this before. Why hadn't I thought to ask?

"When he passed, I was heartbroken and terrified that you might get sick too. That it was some fungus, amoeba, or genetic disease that hadn't been found yet. But you were the perfect spirit of health. I didn't take his death well, and I threw myself into work instead of being there for you, with you. I hired nannies to raise you in my stead, and for a while I was getting better. I was healing, I was going to cut back my hours when your first nanny got sick. I noticed her hands shaking, and she had been so tired. I was shocked, terrified, so I gave her some money to take some time off and moved us across the country for a job," I couldn't breathe. This couldn't be right. How did I not notice?

"Then the next nanny fell ill, and I did the same thing, again and again I gave them money and moved you until your last nanny. Maddie's little girl got sick. She died, Brenna. Just like your father, and I didn't want to see. Then you went to school, and everything was normal for a few years. You got depressed, and started seeing your school counselor, and I thought we were finally past our line of bad luck. Then I got a letter in the mail from your school, letting us know that Mr. Goldstein was taking that leave of absence. Then the next letter came, telling me he'd passed.

"After that, I looked up your old nannies. Every last one had passed. Every person that you touched, really touched in your life had died, and I had finally remembered that dream at the cross roads. The dream with the demon. I did not have to pay the price, but there was a price. He visited me once more, the suit—disheveled —the dream, a nightmare. He smiled at me, and asked how my darling baby girl was doing.

"He thanked me for bringing one of his creatures into this world. A creature that wasn't fully whole, a creature that wasn't fully human. He told me that the price for your survival depended on you... taking it away from others. People are wary of you, Brenna, because you're a predator. They know you're dangerous, so they have walls up. If people let you in, even a little, you just... syphon off whatever makes them, them until they wither away to husks.

"Your father, your nannies, your fiancé, those poor people let you into their lives and you've used them up. My letters come from a fake address. You've been my demon, my curse, my albatross to bear, and I'm so, so sorry I brought you into this world.

"Please, don't call me again. I'm sorry," she hung up.

I stared at the phone, as my mind caught up. This entire time I chose to view my story as the underdog, the weak protagonist, struggling against misfortune heroine. I had not considered that I had control of my tale, that this entire time I had power.

I am a monster.

Setting the phone down, I stripped off my clothes and showered. I let myself mourn. I let it all out, and I prepared.

Hair still dripping, I packed my laptop, some clothes, made arrangements for Brant and flew several states away to try and sever the distance between us. The distance wasn't the issue, it was my hunger and my connection with him. That night, last night, I dreamed, and found my answer.

Many answers, all from a man in a pinstripe suit. I am so happy I packed my laptop. I am quite pleased this hotel has free wifi.

I've discovered that my dreams do touch people. I am not oil in water or a repellant force. Instead, I knock people down like dominos, one after the other, after the other. I am the architect, I can save Brant. I just needed you.

Words are a clever invention, really. They're a voice in your head. A waking dream, almost. My voice is inside your head, my story tucked behind your eyes. I'm inside you now.

As we get older, we think that getting tired is the normal course of aging. We all take on too much sometimes, and being tired may be a sign to take a vacation. When you get tired, I highly recommend you take that vacation, enjoy that peace and those memories. You won't have much time. I will not save you. I need it, I need so many things. Most of all I need Brant. You're just a faceless being looking down at the page.

xx

# About The Authors

# AA Peterson

AA Peterson is some guy who lives in Idaho.

*The Pancake Family* will also be to appearing in an upcoming collection entitled "The Family of Fang and Claw."

Visit aapeterson.com or Facebook.com/ TheDorkKnightReturns for more information about AA Peterson.

---

# Max Lobdell

The stories of Max Lobdell are strategies against

happiness. A prolific author of physical horror, his work will slip inside you, only to claw itself out with little concern for the wreckage it leaves behind. Max's themes are unsettling, bizarre, seductive, and relatable. He writes to make you feel terrible.

You can find more out about Max by visiting his website: unsettlingstories.com. He posts to Reddit under the handle /u/iia.

---

# James "DexX" Dominguez

James has spent two decades as a professional wordslinger in the diverse capacities of technical writer, editor, publisher, digital content creator, playwright, and journalist, but currently is devoting his creative energy toward writing short stories and a possible novel. He lives in Melbourne, Australia.

Visit dexx.com.au to find out more about James. He posts to Reddit under the handle /u/MCDexX.

---

# Rona Vaselaar

Rona Vaselaar is a Minnesota native and grew up surrounded by local urban legends and tall tales. Introduced to horror at an early age, she quickly grew attached to the genre and most of her reading and writing has centered around gruesome stories. She is an alumni of the University of Notre Dame and is planning to attend Johns Hopkins University for graduate school.

You can find her posting to Reddit under her /u/ SleepyHollow_101 handle.

---

# Nina LaRocca

Nina posts to Reddit under her handle, /u/walpurgisnight.

---

# SnollyGolly

SnollyGolly is a writer who pushes the boundaries of genres and is never limited to a single platform.

If you enjoyed his story, you can dive deeper down his rabbit hole by visiting this post: evilmousestudios.com/immersive-horror-through-web-technologies/.

---

# Jacob Healey

Jacob is a 23-year-old writer. When he's not making up stories, he's reading, playing basketball, or watching Netflix with his hot wife. Sometimes he does all of those things simultaneously.

You can find him posting to Reddit under his /u/Sergeant_Darwin handle, and he is building his Facebook page at Facebook.com/thejakehealey.

---

# Nick Botic

Nick Botic is an aspiring writer from Milwaukee, WI. His lifelong passions for all things horror and writing met in late 2015. Since then, he has been churning out story after story, with the ultimate goal of publishing a full length horror novel, as well as an anthology featuring all of his short stories.

Visit <u>nickbotic.com</u> and <u>facebook.com/ nickboticsshortstories</u> for more information. Nick posts to Reddit under the user name of /u/Nickbotic.

———————

# Katie Irvin Leute

Katie is a yoga and dance instructor, studio owner, metal smith and designer. She's spent her life on the lookout for magic amulets, child-like empresses, acorns that turn things to stone, puppy-faced luck dragons, haunted swords, iocane powder, and enchanted roses under every bell jar. While looking for real magic in the world, she makes things that could be magic, with her own hands and some respectfully-borrowed stardust.

To find out more about Katie, you can visit her above mentioned businesses at the following sites: <u>alchemieadornment.com</u> and <u>coilspokane.com</u>. She posts to Reddit under the handle /u/shortCakeSlayer.

---

# FromWarwick

FromWarwick is an anomaly in the horror community. You can find them posting to Reddit under their handle, /u/FromWarwick.

23515057R00171

Printed in Poland
by Amazon Fulfillment
Poland Sp. z o.o., Wrocław